CORRIDOR DANCE

by

Peter Preston

'Corridor Dance' is dedicated to the memory of my father.

CORRIDOR DANCE

Bloomsbury-Alpha Press
London, 2016.
verticaline@hotmail.com

ISBN: 978-1-291-87522-5

PART ONE

CHAPTER ONE

Light is falling onto my friends' faces. Sunlight reddens Peter's and gilds Theo's: it burnishes their faces. Christopher and David hide from the sun and the gravestones shield them. I have to lie alone on the delicate grass.

"What strikes you as important – from when you first came?" asks Peter, and in his eyes are reflected the towers of the cathedral, the sun, a bright summer day. But he is thinking of my Ruth; of the university and all the while of my Ruth. It is kind of him, in the warmth of summer gently to recall her to me. For in this way he brings out my happiness, my fondness here in the graveyard.

But I am wayward. And when this summer's sun burns and burrows – now – through my shirt and onto my chest, and plays at my throat, as the five of us lie here idly, I am all the while thinking of the walk from Shincliffe and to Reverend Ashley's church service; of the mist that deadens the sounds from the fields; and of the world which is circularly white – of which I can see, just a dozen paces.

There is Peter, footfalls sounding dully. His jeans are narrow, clinging, wrinkled at the backs of the knees. The paces fall heavily onto the gravel. As they stop, the jacket which is dark and partly dampened droops slightly forward. It is opened, it is blue. The mist is freezing and on the stones a glaze glistens. It is winter. He beckons and I approach with breath clouded to see the puddle – which is frozen – the pattern of ice-ferns on the surface of the ice, and the bubbles that are below the ice – that is down at his feet.

"Look at this." His very first words – and marking them the bubbles have suddenly shifted – they moved and coalesced under the pressure of his shoe – and his speech came quickly and the bubbles fled. Spaced, particulate, they made way for the cracks. So that what seems important now is the muddiness that surged softly upward and the rejection of the church service. For as I remember it, Peter, we did not go. Instead there was the walk by the river: paces on frozen leaves and the steep banks sloping down – one hundred, two hundred feet – small paths and the race towards the bottom where ice fringed the river. And by that river there is a stone wall; it is a wall that Theo remembers so fixedly that now, anxious, he would like to speak. But Peter's voice runs on. He speaks of the early days and reminds us of things that are fearful to behold and have become, with the passage of time, crystalline.

Peter continues:

"Everything glistened when we came upon that drystone wall down by the river on the first day in the university. Only later did it become labyrinthine. So that as we walked from that wall to the student centre we sensed at once unpleasant friendliness, the trappings of happiness – disfigurement – and a single kind and genuine face. As you looked about the room, insisting upon your status and drawing small antagonisms from every silence, Laura befriended you, she spoke freely."

"Yes, but I was right! There were eyes everywhere and the less than obvious designs."

Theo nods his agreement. Uneasy thoughts rise to threaten us, we feel exposed.

Theo recalls the wall to me. It is mottled – slate and granite together. It is lonely, vulnerable; a northern drystone wall. And he describes my eyes then – cast down; my face – pressed hard against the mottled surface and the tears which on that occasion were shed for Jane, though the wind which is cold raises tears too, it chaps the lips, lays ice on the pond, numbs the venous blood and can cause, too, friends to withdraw.

Theo: "You, abandoned Jane or so it seemed, for at that moment she was dismissed from your mind and Ruth who had a finer mien was then caught up, embraced, warmed by the sun and thrust towards love, to happiness."

"So it was you who stood by me there?"

"Yes, it was. For the honest citizens, the clear-hearted students passed you by. They ignored the tears shed by a stranger and so I too allowed myself the only gentleness of too many years for I dried Jane's own tears, kicked a loosened stone casually, and forgetting everything else, walked silently home."

But there are five of us now, here in the graveyard, so that Christopher, who has brought us all here – to the shade of the cedar trees – stands up. He speaks: it is his story of the earth.

"When I was younger . . ." he begins and David smiles, "I lived in Highgate and worked at the cemetery. I had a companion so that the two of us worked moving earth from each derelict grave to the deserted part of the graveyard. This earth was heavy and black: it seemed pregnant, so that out of undue fear we never worked alone. As we dug, emptying each pit, leaves fell from above and the rain, too, came forcefully in.

"In this position I had a special fear, but my friend with great determination pressed on with our task. So it was that when we came to remove an unwanted tree stump it was I whose sight fell upon what the rain and my friend's brave gestures had not fully revealed – for lying beneath us were the broken remains of a man's wooden box.

"And my friend struck out and the root came away. He pulled, and with the root came faith and hope and a final agony. He pulled and as he leant back – straining – the earth and everything unknown tilted too. And fluid ran out and the weight inside slid down – and the wooden box, which had waited eighty years to greet the day, found the crisp air altogether too much for it, and the bump onto the ground far too much for it, so that in an earthly birth, the broken coffin split. And I at last was able to see the destruction of one man's faith, his hope: in one brief moment I looked to see that the corpse's skin was plainly black like leather – the flesh, alive with crawling life was whitened like cream."

CHAPTER TWO

Yet here in Durham it is beautiful. There are bridges – Elvet, Kingsgate, Prebends – woods and woodland flowers, and there are crisp sounds, too, from the watermill, from the weir.

And the cathedral sits and glowers over us all and the town which is caught in the sun floats imperceptibly, light dispelling the shadows, so that in the ancient streets the sunlight falls hotly and for the most part it is bright and wholesome day. In this way, if there is a threat at all, then it must run in the small places – in the tiny squares where passageways meet.

From our position in the graveyard we are well placed to hear muffled cries from the bridge – from Prebends. Christopher, having told his tale rises. He makes off slowly in the direction of the noise. Those who are left are David and Theo and Peter who is talking to me now. It is as if Ruth were here.

We look up. We are to be dazzled by a smile, by the rigours of academic discipline, the strictures of fashion and the pretty legs that she will cross for me. On this bright summer day we are to be blinded at once by full sexual display.

Ruth *is* here.

From a few feet above us the world is upset by beauty, and

from there a thrill spreads through the air so that the leaves which dip with their branches immediately become green, the earth which holds such a special appeal for Christopher becomes brown and the wall surrounding us all becomes low and stone-coloured. It becomes grey. Spreading outward from her transitory smile – that English moment – is her warmth which I call love and she speaks her first words:

"May I sit down?"

Birds can be heard, the sun lights the highest clouds with gold and hearts suddenly lift. Beneath our feet, burrowing and crawling animals devour their young.

Sounds are suddenly heard from the river. Straightaway David leaps to his feet. Ruth who has made the circle radiant turns her head. Cries stretch angrily from away across the town and now, from Kingsgate Bridge crowds are cheering and shouting fearful oaths. And David who is gesturing, is stiff and strained – he is soon to be gone. Apart from Ruth three students remain.

So now the first pageant through the city begins and Theo and Peter lead the way – wordlessly, strangely holding their heads quite low – so that only occasionally can their faces be seen by Ruth or myself who follow, though not closely, nor even together.

We pass through the town: behind us the campus and the castle, and we move to a small street cut off from the light. In the street, the houses which are tall nearly reach together and close tightly on the sky.

Theo wants to move in the direction of Dunelm House and there is some connivance with Peter.

"Where's that crowd going? Can you see?" asks Peter who is nearest to the vennel which gives onto the high banks of the river. For he feels it is important to know where such a crowd might be going, especially one that breaks out now and then into rhythmic shouting; since it cheers, cries, breathes a protest, is suddenly silent – like the moment which follows lightning and precedes thunder – so that all of this occurs oddly in a street which glares at one. Glares: so that it is felt that there alone in the dust – near to a broken doorway, among piles of filing cabinets – is the brightly lit spot where something decisive did once suddenly happen.

Peter: "To the river!"

"Yes, we can do it quickly!"

"Yes! Now let's go!"

Glad, the three of us set out. We step – rapidly to the vennel entrance. In a single movement, with lightness of heart so that it is seen to be the one, speedy and inevitable move. Ruth remains.

"Quick! To the river!"

"Forward to the towpath!"

"Never look back!"

And Peter and Theo rush on. And I am lost – somehow – in the crowd. My mind runs on:

There was a time – another time – when Ruth went missing, and as these bright young people – not as beautiful as she is – rush past us now, it is that occasion which comes to mind: it stops me rigid. I stand back to think.

I had grown to trust Ruth – her smiles, the odd moments of repose – when on taking her examinations she suddenly disappeared altogether. This was a cruel expediency, for she left without a word. Something, however, had driven me to the doctor's that day: a pain – my septic foot; some other disorder – my epilepsy; or perhaps the kind doctor, who took notes in shorthand on all his patients, perhaps this man drew inner pain toward him in the way of a rich man and his beggars or of a spider and its prey.

In his surgery, I imagine, I am now well hidden. Hunched, wilful, hesitating to speak: fearing the doctor's diligent attention, his record, too, of every word that I speak. A delicate rain falls outside and sunlight streams through the largest of the windows. The view from the window is of Shire Hall, the centre of university administration, and of the low wall which surrounds Dunelm House – surrounds too, the medical centre, the surgery within the medical centre and the fine cane chair which is where I now sit.

The doctor looks across the room. He glances through the window – he glances at the Vice-Chancellor's office, the Vice-Chancellor himself, and the slight, pretty secretary caught up in bright dreams. Although the view between the two men is unimpeded, so far, their eyes have never, ever met. The doctor returns to my gaze.

He speaks: "I can assume, I hope, that your work is going quite well?"

"Yes," I reply. "But Ruth . . ."

"Is she one of my patients? Is she in my files somewhere?"

"No."

"Are *you* ill then?" His face makes some expression of profound concern. A warm ocean. The doctor is handsome, perhaps middle-aged. The way he smiles, the smart grey of his suit, the professional manner that he uses; all this is called to his aid straightaway, for the clever doctor was having difficulty in concealing – carefully – that through lack of suffering, the doctor could not care.

And what transpired was unacceptable: there was no refining fire. To this man unversed in anguish, and free, beneath a discerning exterior, of all human frailty, I brought the disgusting – those things truly to be called mawkish for my thoughts had become errant and Ruth's beauty was making its demands of me. It shrieked, so that I too would cry out loud. It demanded: what was mere speech – this vain subtle act – when the room and the whole world might be shifted; when they might have slipped eventually, and slid gloriously away?

And what was left of myself was maudlin, inadequate.

Tearful, I was unable to face the steel in the eye of medical philanthropy, of the doctor. He leant forward.

"There's something else?" And he wrote out a prescription for my epilepsy, he coolly lanced my livid abscess.

"Yes, yes!" And tears flowed. They cried out to heaven for the redress of wrongs and the doctor wrote in his notes: *something else*. He thought evenly: there is something else.

But what I was able to relate was humiliating: I could say I missed Ruth; nothing more. I missed her and as a result I was crying with no thought of my shame and in front of a doctor who was thinking:

"A man should be able to hold himself upright. Not give way, not give way at all!"

And so I was an unworthy and a womanly youth. I was a shallow vessel, a flaccid and a broken stem. This soft and docile warrior cried out for help when none was needed: he was broken and was glad to be so. And the doctor would have no part in any indulgence. He would look at me with white light – with reason – and because he wanted, the doctor said, to relieve pain wherever he might, he would spend a little time – a few arid moments – and I could be glad in my stillness, and in my secret ways and in the night.

But in the end what was to cause the day to slip away; what he said – recorded in my file – was yet to shock me. For Ruth, who is beautiful and is said to love me; Ruth, who had gathered just a few friends about her – she is said to be admirable only by those who are her close relatives – Ruth, viewed impartially by a general practitioner might appear – truly – as nothing but faithless. And the doctor sensed this. And such was the strength of the white light that he brought to bear, that on that sad occasion I actually agreed.

So it was that this tearful vessel assented – for the doctor clearly was seen to be writing: *tied to unfaithful girlfriend*. And when he closed his notes he put away the file so that, summarily, what now chills the perceptions, freezes the skin, is the single dark and monstrous truth: strangely, the vain and shallow doctor was nevertheless *right*.

CHAPTER THREE

The crowd is drawing me onto the bridge.

There is splashing and shouting, a large banner and a crowd further ahead. There are flags on high parapets. And they overhang the river. The banner and flags are painted: roughly with gold lettering. As the wind lifts them, the sky – blue with grey clouds – glints through coloured linen.

Overhead birds fly, down below eight oars strike out: a long boat is floundering. This boat is beetle-like, crab-like, a giant insect. The oars thrash out and water tumbles from above.

"What's happening here?"

"Look! Fire hoses! Fire hoses on the bridge!"

And a crowd throwing rubbish. From seventy feet it tumbles – from Kingsgate Bridge alongside Dunelm House – from where the banners twist and where the large windows of an assembly hall glisten.

"It's a demonstration!"

"You can't go in! Not into Dunelm House!"

There was contempt in the air. Contempt for a strange movement, its occupation of a building – there was nothing more – and if you looked closely, you would see that as might be expected all the faces carried with them the exclusive hope of an extreme burden.

But the issue would surely be decided soon. The rowing eight had, quite intentionally, broken through the cordon round Dunelm House – though meeting with its difficulties in the shadow of the bridge. And now defiance and arrogance were met with petulance and cunning, for there was no more splendid way to sink this boat than with five fire hoses – and with giant arcing jets and rainbows.

But by the bridge a vast crowd had assembled and the banks, a hundred feet high, were now being trampled so that henceforth there would be no shrubs, no summer flowers and the few fences would be crushed as the crowd clamoured – immensely, suddenly, intent upon the bridge.

All about police vans could be seen. Journalists and photographers rushed from the nearest copse to join small battles at the cordon. But the police held their line and thus the protective shell was saved. I was amazed at the size of the movement so rapidly arisen. I was, too, at the response: that floodlights should be installed, that all entrances and exits should be covered, that those entering should be photographed and in this way identified. And I was amazed, as well, that this unusual conceit had remained for so long in such secrecy.

But the rest of the crowd was not surprised: one man, turning to meet me, seemed to speak directly with his eyes. He watched all my reactions and he would have made to get alongside me, but for the crush. And so I was left with not an uncomfortable feeling, but instead one of great mystery.

A cry. Eyes fix on the cox of the eight. His boat which is sinking to its gunwales responds to his command.

"Quick! Pull together!"

"Quick! To the banks!"

If they begin now, if they manage to pull away without sinking at either the stern or the prow; if they move from the bridge's shadow and steadily, safely, from the threat of the cascades; if they show the crowd that it is right to ignore an illicit cordon, an unheard-of movement – then it will be proved right to challenge all such strange activity. And all of their efforts would be excellent of course.

Reaching to left and right they made their first heavy move to the nearest bank, while John and Maurice pulled steadily and Stephen, who is president of the union, pulled heavily: they made for the bank.

But just as the crowd decided to applaud their success; had found it good and orderly – correct in one's attitude to limit one's purview to courtly love, to historicism, to vector analysis, to physics; just as all this turned out casually to be true, a fearful event occurred because just then a dustbin lit a fine curve from the dissidents' bridge, tumbled seventy feet and crushed – nearly – the cox's shape. It certainly wrecked the stern.

The crash was not really heard. Spray rose and fell, wood splintered and people cried out: those in the water struggled in fear – two had leapt from the sides – but cries reached upward and as I saw the boat settling, a small face in the crowd turned purposefully toward me once more.

The oars moved tragically as the hoses turned fully onto the stern. The water filled the boat so that finally it began to sink and all that remained was the row of torsos – an incomplete array – and as those who were screaming cut, parted the air, I rushed through the bulrushes and a slight amount of mud to help and to save whomever I could.

In the water everything is cold. The mud is cloying and my clothes smother me – they are a soft, wet grip. Clearly I must strike out, I must be rid of impediments: I will discard these clothes and they will float downstream.

Stephen is struggling but nevertheless manages to direct his crew.

"Swim for cover!" And again more bravely: "Swim!"

But not everyone will have heard this cry: Ian who is holding onto the stern can have had no time for a reply. But John who drifts past – choking beneath the surface – John clutches for my ankle and in this private extreme, he is most silent of all.

The cox is close and must be quick. He arches away: he inverts. He slides straight down in the water and grasps for John's shirt before I can reach some little way: to grasp first a leg and then a shoulder. What follows is his left arm, his left side; and straightaway the coughing of water and of blood. We move him heavily to the shore.

At the bank he becomes calmed. John no longer fights so that his vomit at last begins to flow – in green, in red, in river-water brown. I stand there nearly naked and the crowd presses about me: Reverend Ashley, jealous for John's soul, is immediately at my side. In the crowd, glances move outward starting from the same small face, perhaps that of a messenger, and an awareness seems to play lightly among the people by the trees – for John has been saved.

Stephen is still perilously adrift. Clutching the tiller and unheedful of his own advice he floats, twisting, his eyes fixed.

But Stephen just rotates. In silence and clutching motionless to his tiny support he gyrates. And the crowd - as each person is caught in the twisting gaze flinches - it falls silently back. Under Stephen's gaze it breathes, sighs variously, and it is thus, as his eyes return again and again, that Stephen drifts slowly from the student throng to the deep-water channel so that motionless – in the end – he is carried straightaway to the weir.

The small-faced figure – he is from Hatfield College and his eyes appear to have settled upon me – approaches silently indicating I am wanted inside the cordon round Dunelm House, Shire Hall and the medical centre itself. I follow him past a small part of the crowd and every last one of the staring faces.

The faces turn suddenly away. David chooses not to

recognise me and somewhere deep in the back Christopher keeps his head fixed, his eyes tightly shut.

I am abandoned by Theo and Ruth and walk, dripping wet and near naked, behind the messenger and up the towpath – over the balustrade and onto Kingsgate Bridge. I walk rapidly past the police, the photographer recording every entry behind the cordon and, in the end, past a crowd of girls: those clustered behind the picket line (they are muses, they are goddesses, they are poor enslaved souls) and I climb up three final steps. To the left and right are the silhouettes of unknown figures. They hold a line. Against the police – matching them man for man, and against the strangely attentive crowd, they maintain their discipline.

But the girls gather round them. They giggle when the police line breaks momentarily and they pay their odd respect to several among the guards' number. I turn to get my clothes.

"Don't be long!" The messenger says, and then adds: "They want to see you inside – and then, of course, there's the question of your file."

But my clothes were in the custody of the police so I returned to the doors of Dunelm House, and peered carefully through – I was, perhaps, an opponent of this movement. Now, facing me, a figure was seated at a table, though the messenger was nowhere to be seen. Seeing the figure, I looked carefully at each of the other faces; perhaps hoping to find him standing among these guards even, possibly, among the police.

But clearly, the messenger had made straight inside. Standing before his fellows, and unlike me, completely unafraid, he would no doubt tell the company where I had been found. He would thus give an altogether strange impression of me and I would be seen as jealous for position – and he would describe me as vacillating at the river side – he would say I was no help at all: no help, that is, until I plunged in, on the pretext of helping my friends, finally to undo the legitimate work. "Simon

Bader," he would say, "is not to be counted among our number!"

But I felt I would have to get my file – in this way to secure the doctor's monstrous discovery recorded within – and so it was that this single fact became my paramount consideration. This surely was something constant – a thing keenly to be held onto. It was never to be forgotten.

And Ruth would not pass from my mind. I was thinking of her as I passed into the hall and down the corridor, lined with candles and other signs of night-time austerity: her beautiful face was held before me as I walked, so that where the interior showed signs of sadness and lack of promise, a fine and shining star was always in view.

I entered one of the rooms. With one gesture I was motioned to come in. I was shown the way with cursory warnings. Here, I thought, I would surely find a reception committee, in all probability it would be waiting here for me.

A strange thought as I opened the door and looked at the cubicles inside: Theo and Peter left out in the crowd – might they not be here already? But, in fact, they were not to be found in any of the cubicles.

Inside were cardboard boxes and stronger wooden cases. The paint on the cubicles was dripping because it had been smeared in places. There were people standing singly and in groups – their clothes stained with too much paint – there was, in fact, the sense of important work going on. And among this crowd – for people thronged the passageway – among the horde I actually felt expected. Just casually, one of the painters pushed me to a cardboard cubicle where a girl was waiting with camera and tripod.

The camera was focused, the plate was set. She adjusted her dress and I felt provoked. Rapidly she switched on a brilliant flood, and by its light I saw conclusively that there was nothing like a reception committee here. Her soft hands aligned my head – my jawline could not be allowed to fall into too much shade – and when the photo was done she smiled indicating that there was now a record for the police, and one for the Vice-Chancellor, there was one, too, for the movement itself.

And the three photos were sent off. Thus were the people outside informed who was involved within the building – and in this way, too, might they then make their retribution certain to the same degree.

But the photographer made no claims for herself. Waving me on down the room she disclaimed her commitment for she suddenly cried out:

"Good heavens, no! Who'd be committed to *this*?"

And it might have been a reply – if, indeed, there had been any question – so I turned to look at the beautiful face of this unerring reader of thoughts. I glanced back at her and touched her gently. She let me glance, she welcomed my touch: she returned it hotly.

But the painters were more frenzied. Moving me to a new cubicle they seemed more concerned with the fact of my arrival than with the need to warn me of their work – the wet paintwork – and of the signalling and gesturing behind my back.

"Have you come with a message for us?" They said and there was an odd obsequiousness in both of their voices – especially as the painters were hiding from, of all people, Laura – Laura who was working some way away and was even now carrying off this, our strange encounter, with a high degree of unearthly calm. I chided the painters on their lack of consideration.

"Will you be giving us new instructions?"

The voice came from the next door booth so that the painters' frenzy sounded like sibilant scratchings on the packing-case wall. (This was the too rapid building of the fabric of the movement. The hurried pursuit of an idea not yet formed.) But in imagining that, of course, the painters would be wrong.

21

"Oh, but it is really quite likely!"

"Yes, for we could imagine someone saying – it would be spoken quite deliberately – 'Simon Bader, tell the painters they're needed in the Great Hall'.

"And the message would perhaps come from someone well-placed: it would be phrased in an *official* way.

"But none of this would ever intimidate you – for a person with your bearing would quite naturally be able to shrug off all such excesses."

I was dumbfounded: "How is that?" I asked, feeling uncomfortable that the unseen painters had now exceeded all deference and wondering, too, how they had known my name.

"Because you're so well known!" They replied, and their fawning dulled the air of conspiracy so I was left with that foreboding more properly reserved for the truly notorious.

The painter continued: "Someone with your reputation should be highly placed and could therefore intercede for us so as to lessen our workload. At the very least, we could hope that new instructions might be received through you and consequently we might be allowed to leave this present work – and so move higher. You see, at present, we must work so fast that before the top coat is dry we must apply the stencils and then write in the lettering: the result is that the paint runs, the letters blur – our work is lost . . ."

But just as they were saying this, a flurry of new people entered the rooms.

"They're interrogators!" One of the painters had leant over to me: it was a last communication.

At this, some new figures moved to the cubicles so that when these others followed them, and a whispering arose, their faces became obscured. They were visible only if one of them moved, thus permitting a clear line of sight from my cubicle – at the very end of one of the rows. A great deal of discussion seemed necessary and the interrogators gathered severally in the corridor and spoke intermittently. In particular, they made very large gestures. Apparently I was to have no interrogator at all.

The painters' brushes made hasty sweeps across the neighbouring wall. By occasional gestures and a strange peering they advised this highly-placed one that silence was very important. "Silence!" They hissed and their brush strokes continued.

I glanced toward the photographer once more. "She's not even a member, you know." The painters were enthusiastic. They signalled to me.

"Why not?" I asked, speaking the words out loud.

"Because she doesn't stay within the building at night!" It seemed uncompromising. And so she seemed of more favoured stuff or perhaps a disquieted soul – unsettled – like myself. Of certainty, I considered, there were her fine legs, the skirt which was enticing; and the light golden hair – she had never been a student, she had smooth and manicured hands – and she smiled at me.

But the tide of bright shimmering surfaces, of delicate, shining silver things delighting the heart, causing the day to be finely set, oneself to be caught rather delicately; all this passed and dear memories entered my mind of another's weak smile as I once passed on my way to the lecture halls. Suddenly, although Laura had seemed to pass out of my life in those first days, and except for the occasional brief and perfunctory meeting, nevertheless, it was she who now stood before me as bold and honest representative of an incomprehensible movement; an adventure. I sat there amazed.

But a painter was to relieve my astonishment. By whispering in my ear he described this venture; he whispered, too, details of Laura's career. He filled in certain gaps.

"Don't be amazed," he began. "The planning for the movement was done long before any of this happened." And the painter illustrated this point graphically: he stretched his delicate hands across his face fitfully – it was a language of gestures.

These hands moved: they told an enormous story so that throughout not one word was ever heard and the many red-eyed and eager listeners sat back incuriously. They hid from my sight, too, filling up completely the cubicle next door.

"It was an enormous task," he began. "Even so, the work, once undertaken, was completed thoroughly so that such is our development that hardly any paperwork remains here inside the building. Everything of importance is kept as a memory. In your case there will probably be a verbal report. More certain still – there will never, ever be another word on paper . . ."

" . . . And this is the reason why individual helpers become intent upon eavesdropping . . ." The painter's companion – David – uncannily answered my unspoken question and I instantly turned round to see if he would do so again.

He did. "The fact," he said, "that we painters were two of the earliest helpers is not a point I would wish to emphasize to Laura's cost."

Likewise he discounted their membership of the committee, their work on the flow diagrams and also their joint proposal on channels of command – which pre-dated Laura's own induction greatly. Again, the present disparity in rank between Laura and themselves, could, he said, be seen as a mere oversight: the fault of otherwise excellent helpers known to the painters, and he went on to add that as soon as the present difficulties were ironed out, they – the painters – expected to be joining the ranks of these higher officials and so David's gestures finished to the prolonged and heartfelt applause of his friend, Christopher, his companion within the movement.

Christopher indicated more. Christopher insisted nothing should be allowed to disturb this friend, Laura. By the same token, he went on, whatever troubled her, hindered the cause –

their true and proper concern. And so, he said, while they remained in her hands – as painters they were to act under the direction of such officials as the interrogators; of the many other members, too – then they were to be satisfied only with Laura's complete contentment.

If their request to me jeopardised any part of the movement, then, Christopher continued, it would be reconsidered and instantly and loyally withdrawn. But equally, as eager associates of the great project, the movement's efficiency was uppermost in their minds and it had thus become some part of their duty to underline the conditions that they, the painters, had had to endure. All this and much, much more they laid – and with a special zeal – at the feet of interrogator Laura.

Laura was silent for some time. Both the painters had stopped and David, who at last was toying with his brush, clearly felt that too much time had already been lost and they must, of necessity be about their duty.

Eventually, the interrogator spoke: it was with sadness, Laura said, that she had heard of the painters' unhappy state. The account she would now be obliged to pass on – albeit not a written one – would emphasize just this spirit of loyalty, of disinterest to the right people and there would, as a consequence, be a restructuring of schedules. Roger, she felt, would prove to be understanding. He was, indeed, the most sympathetic of her contacts within.

But, continuing to work, the painters now ignored her. Nodding gracefully, and not stopping her flow for the slightest of moments, she addressed her closing remarks in a new direction. She spoke clearly and evenly and directly towards me.

"Simon!" She said out loud. "Suspicion simply clings to your name!" And then more calmly she said, as if to herself: "Perhaps, too, it penetrates some way into the project."

But I was an erring newcomer once more. I was defenceless.

To myself I cried: "Think of your fine words on the day we met!"

I wanted to turn from the interrogator's sanction, wanted to bask – like the painters – in some degree of acceptance, of tolerance, because I was not even sure why I had come.

"We are not even sure why you have come!" Laura said. Her words were amplified with gestures which were small, precise, difficult to emulate, but still a subtle and fluid language of their own. "So we must question you and thus decide upon a priority for you. We must complete our assessment of all you have done before you came to the project."

"Well," I began, remembering Laura's original question, "you know I was sent for by the committee. . ."

But Laura turned an impatient face away from me. In fact, in her need to express her exasperation, she looked towards the painters briefly and unintentionally so David and Christopher were heartened by this unexpected inclusion: dutifully they shared her irritation. Certainly, all unseen, they exhibited Laura's own haughtiness, the same disdain.

"But surely you realize there is no such thing here as a committee?" Laura said and went on in low tones – tones designed to gather applause from every quarter - to make her exposition.

I sat back and listened. Laura went on: I was right, perhaps to have looked upon the great project as something somehow akin to a movement – but that was only permissible when separated from the clear air of present reasoning. Now that I was within the building there was, she said, the refining effect of fine inner contact and thus the brave exploit, the project, ought to be recognised for what it is – and the endeavour was clearly an agent of the subtlest changes. Henceforth, out of this light, civilising force there would be a grand design, a rising hope; full and ample day: a new sun.

And the sunlight shone brightly on Laura. All at once I was

26

held in her confidential embrace.

"I have hopes for you," she said, "hopes which far exceed those I once held for these two friends – present imbeciles, these painters who peer stupidly at us from behind the partitioning. And so it is imperative that you guard, as we all do, against laxities in thought and in speech. For such laxities could harm the fabric of our great project – and it is for this reason that there are certain safeguards, a language of gestures." But she broke off quickly as another thought came into her mind:

"Perhaps you could give me a description of the messenger who summoned you here and preferably, too, of the person who mentioned that offensive description in the first place? Then again, someone may have recognised one of you – especially as you're so wet and unclothed as yet. Or else this guide might come forward of his own accord?"

"Either way, it will help to establish your own sincerity, which at this moment, is greatly in doubt. I have not been able to proceed further with your interrogation than this first question, but still, the answer that was given was so disturbing that to go beyond this single point would be impossible. I need not say how disastrously this upsets my hopes for you . . . but still, we will return to this matter at some later time.

"And of course it will be absolutely necessary for your good intentions to be recognized before anything more takes place. Perhaps, in the meantime, we can ask something of you – something that will help us to accept your sincerity – if that is what eventually proves to be necessary."

The task was to be a simple one: Laura looked down at the floor, she frowned.

"Good and aspiring helpers would never leave a floor looking like this . . ." and she indicated the interrogation rooms, the doorway and the corridor outside. She made a scrubbing motion with her hand, she gestured *mop* and again, *bucket* and she pointed to the puddles of water which had formed at my feet.

I was embarrassed but I was eager. I made my assurances and indicated clearly that I would clean up all the mess and straightaway too. I showed I could be relied upon absolutely and that I would take the industrious painters as my mentors so that everything would henceforth be done to ensure the smooth running of the excellent movement. And all of this took place amid nods and smiles, amid the delicate approval, the assurances of my listeners. It took place, too, while the vivid image of my own half-naked form – in the company of the messenger – passed, in my mind, up the steps and across the barricades, while it moved among painters, interrogators – and those delicate, scornful, simpering girls.

But the image was cut off. It was suddenly cast out for some natural order existed, some gulf was placed between us so that of course my companion was assumed higher – there perhaps to lose all knowledge of me – though perhaps, too, to return to the crowd again and again – so that the messenger might be a shining light within the movement, clearly a fine worker, a true friend, he was especially an unknown and elusive hope.

Laura continued: "Your messenger is the only person who can verify what you say." And I saw how important it was that someone did. It was important for Ruth and our love and those few rare moments: because a doctor knows faithless Ruth's secret, has written it down – in Dunelm House – and because events have overtaken this record and threaten, therefore, a terrible confidence.

And especially so for coarse investigating eyes penetrating this file might threaten therefore its secrecy. And I cannot bear to look at this love, except fondly; certainly not for too long.

But there is Theo and there is Peter and they have moved towards the barricades. Laura is speaking:

"You are entitled, on my authority to stay for one day," she looked down, "but by tomorrow you must have established the truth of what you say. As of this moment you are here upon no proven invitation and with the worst of all possible histories: Stephen, the river, and with a too close association with what is unacceptable outside."

But Laura smiled as she said this: it was as if some discussion was necessary and she went on to describe the setting up of the movement and thus to explain the ensuing need for caution.

"It is a great task we are undertaking here," she said, "and those who were present at the outset gave everything so that others might benefit. In the first place there were those working with the initial concept and who struggled, through the weeks and months, worked so that they finally established what is our theoretical base – and I cannot begin to tell you what an awful fate eventually overcame them. And then there are the guards charged with resolutely forcing back any opposing momentum, so as ultimately to form this movement. They forged our hope.

"We who now work on the inside must bear their aspirations bravely, we must work for the common good. It is my task – as interrogator – to examine the accounts of those who aspire to join us, so I have found that all kinds of dubious people nowadays flock to our side. It is a fact that many of the keenest adherents who perhaps hold genuinely to our ideals were nevertheless inexplicably missing during the trying times before the establishment of our bridgehead. It must be said that while we welcome their sympathy we must, even so, question the motives of those who took no pains to seek us out when the arduous early work was being done.

"Now in your case it may be that there are those within our ranks who will have a special interest in you – this may not be the case, I merely suggest that it might be so – and such individuals might have formed a favourable view. Again, I can't say, but you yourself will be able to judge if your motivation corresponds to what you feel to be ours.

"Bear in mind that you appear to us only imperfectly, so we can judge only from externals. We do see, however, someone near naked, still wet from giving succour to our opponents and responsible, perhaps, for a death in a confrontation down by the river."

I looked straight ahead. Laura had finished now and she was staring at me. The painters whose appearances were becoming strangely familiar, and more so every second, they too had stopped and their eyes penetrated deep into mine. (While on the floor a pool of white grew with every drop from their brushes, which they held casually as if the floor – the preserve of carpenters and cleaners – was, in fact, no concern of theirs.)

A fearsome attention was turned suddenly upon me. Question and answer gave way to an unblinking stare. It was as piercing as a lizard's. Gripped by sudden fear I rushed for the door. But the others, these scaly beings, these lizards were spilling out with me so that the passageway was completely blocked as I stepped over bags placed in my path. I wound my way to the door and to the corridor outside. Though fearful of a reptile's touch, I nevertheless squeezed between two sturdy questioners, so that forced to plead with the girls who sat close to the doorway – the only people not clamouring for the exit – to plead for light, air and salvation; I ran from the lizard's nest. I fled down the corridor to greet the outer air and the massed crowds still clinging to the paths that led away from Dunelm House. With eyes smarting I cursed the girls' ethereal beauty, their evident freedom, and perhaps, too, some of their disdain.

But there was a sudden noise and someone's voice behind me. The girl photographer standing some way beyond the cordon gestured that she would get my clothes.

"I want to do something for you!" She said. And her determination was a small and revealing gesture and her light, friendly air was happy. I gave her my hand.

"I've already done *one* thing!" She said, and passed me a

crumpled photograph: "Here's one of your arrival." Then again: "Now if I hold your arm we can go to the police van."

We moved through the crowds. Her small voice sounded happy as she made her assurances about my safety and about all of my clothes. This was a welcome interlude. Throughout, on our journey, she told me how beautifully my photograph had come out and her requests for my assistance became stranger and more excited still.

"Perhaps there will be still more interesting people for us to meet!" And she picked her way through crowds who handed me my clothes – one by one – whenever a slight inclination of her head indicated that it was time to do so.

"You can come to Shire Hall and get changed there," she said as I followed her to the offices of the administration centre – cool, disturbing – and through the typing pool, the examination department, and so many other doors (half opened and watched over by elderly secretaries and by others who might yield - because of their youth – and who might smile if an excited glance came just once in their direction). And along corridors which fade into darkness and down which people disappear, as the young secretaries disappear, and along corridors which are green and cream and eventually on towards the post-room.

"This is my room," she said with no trace of an explanation. For the girl had never been a student, was in fact, on the Vice-Chancellor's staff and only worked in Dunelm House by virtue of a certain agreement of interests.

"But that's not odd!" The photographer claimed, for she was recognized everywhere as evidence of a deal between Dunelm House and the university, was known as a free agent and thus managed to pass easily from one to the other, and was, as a consequence, a bright and unfettered spirit, and was perhaps doubly blessed. (And the movement was a nine-day wonder, an indeterminate and rashly formed organization, a pretentious band of visionaries, a single desperate ship of fools.)

31

"But they're there," she said, "and while they themselves need records and while the Vice-Chancellor needs photographs of the sympathisers I shall always continue my work. Especially as the movement makes every claim now that it cannot fail."

I silenced her quickly: "What is your name?"

And she replied: "Samantha." So that I could hold her hand and call her by name and ignore the titters from simpering typists, and thus I clutched my pile of clothes carefully and held onto my shoes tightly – they did not fall – and so I showed the minimum of discomfort; for the small crowd of onlookers was following and questioning and whispered gently – and were it not for the Vice-Chancellor's waiting room there would have been no hiding place at all.

We entered the room. "You can make love to me now if you like," she said, not turning round but instead waving slightly from the window to the doctor in his surgery. I remained silent, I fingered my clothes, I thought wistfully of Ruth.

And this was my shame. Reaching for the key and turning it, locking out the press of the crowd – it had followed me from outside – and turning the blinds so that my body betrayed Ruth heedlessly. On the floor with the dusty air in my breath Samantha's body became pliant.

Question:

"Was this a special day for me that I should be singled out from the crowd; that I should be taken by a messenger so disgraced by his origins that he disappeared rather than say the word *Hatfield* out loud?" (A word which had set several interviews back to faltering re-starts. For those sitting close to me had looked at me with shocked eyes and with sharply indrawn breath – at the culprit who had not shaken off the dust of the university and instead dragged himself across a sterile Dunelm House floor to say: "I think he came from Hatfield College".)

32

And question:

"Will there be friends? Friends to shield me from the prying eyes; from Stephen's dead eyes, and shall I be confronted with the doctor's secret; Theo, Peter and Ruth, and at last some darkening peril from the movement itself?" (And tonight, may the moth fly too close to the flame, enter it and be consumed by its light?)

And Samantha replied slowly:

"Oh no, my darling!"

And question:

"Did I kill Stephen? Did I stab, suffocate, slash or drown him secretly? Did I falter, swim too weakly, or render him at last, insufficient aid?"

"Oh no my darling! You could not, my darling. But you are, my sweet, the rarest of gifts: you were on that occasion, knowing and a trifle confused. You were prepared, somehow, because you turned up naked. You were safe from all dangers that were lying there waiting.

"Dangers that lay there giggling and waiting, wielding paint brushes and waiting, spying and making out reports and waiting, drying rain-soaked, grave-soiled clothes and waiting. Dangers that lay there waiting for you – you who turned up especially safe, freed from their smears – safe in fact, because you turned up naked.

"Naked."

Later I asked Samantha about the movement.

"There is something bleak about its very centre. Tell me, Samantha, what is it I have to fear?"

But Samantha was in no mood to give a direct reply. "Entry into the centre. Penetration too far."

Her eyes caught the light from the windows – a hundred dust motes in the air. We lay back, we made love once more and when we got dressed we walked down by the river and we talked a lot more:

"How did it start, Samantha?"

"The movement? I don't think I could tell you. It would take all day."

CHAPTER FOUR

Down by the river with the crowd dispersed, I turned to Samantha, I was to tell her my tale. The sun caught the trees, grass was pressed down and the river flowed brown. It flowed heavily. The signs of the departed crowds covered the landscape. It was an afternoon illuminated by sunshine – silence and ripples – it was bright with memories; and there was too, the recollection of the sun playing among the waves on a river; of a host of small and tranquil things which pass fleetingly on an afternoon which is glistening, and is, perhaps, radiant like this.

A young man, standing alone, glides in a low, flat boat in this day's clear sunshine. He has seen the river on many afternoons: it was brittle during winter's rigid quiescence, and he can follow the water's signs as it moves – but almost secretly – so that the boat causes the first real waves for some time. Certainly the first of this afternoon.

He stands erect and looks at the prow. He pauses – and as the pole glides straight down, some small quality of beauty seems added to him, for it would be hard for him not to be noticeable on a day which is so bright; on an afternoon such as this.

His hands become wet as he lifts the pole out of the water. The wood, which is softened, glistens with water drops. He wears no shoes and his feet leave wet patches – the varnish dries quite rapidly and he rapidly shifts his feet – he is constantly pushing, constantly guiding.

And the day itself is perfectly blue. The noises all about are from unseen couples, carried with a certain wistfulness from across the water. As the punt drifts on, the sky becomes narrowed for the banks begin to tower and their tall trees loom overhead. The sun yellows their still leaves into a canopy – it yellows them thus, but not fully.

Someone is waiting for him. A girl – she is only just ready – waves so that the boat takes a new tack and the traces turn in on themselves. Amid his silence, the young man makes for the jetty so that at last eyes meet, voices murmur and hands, too, can clasp their greeting.

They talk of summer things; they speak of friends not now present. They glide from the landing – she is a sheen of pinkness, she has light golden hair – and where the water swirls over humped island weeds, he gently frames a question. Straightaway she replies.

She speaks:

> *"I lie here. I rest and my body is tense with the knowledge of you. I lie here in a secret way with just the image of my love on a day which is perfectly blue. Blue now that the wind has dropped. I feel you part my hair with the hand which I long to touch. Now is the time when my body is open, now is the time when I shimmer, wishing to give but constrained to wait. The sun has opened my eyes. The wind which passes round the tops of the trees with low sounds has opened my ears to you and I wait for you to speak. I sing with the circling wind for you, you who have opened all this with your eyes.*

Look into my eyes and see that I am willing to give. Look into me and see that my voice is soaring with the circling wind, that my arms enfold a world in their embrace on a day which is perfectly blue. See that I love on an afternoon such as this."

"Yes, I see your eyes with the sun reflected in them. I grasp towards you; I am cold, I am exposed. Look at me for I tremble, I tremble on an afternoon such as this."

"Let us not stay, for the sun will dip low and the redness will fill the branches of the trees. The sunset will end what the wind and the light on the water have made for us. And I will make memorable this day for you; so that when we return I will show you that I can give of myself and again give."

And the river is yet lonelier.

"Shall we stop now? Shall we find some small untrodden beach? Shall we head the boat towards its beaching; will you rest with me and feel cold sparkling on wet feet – shall we do this and shall we pause? (Will you walk with me through green rushes, wading knee-deep in this gliding water – will you perch on slippery rocks – laughing, feeling my gladness?)"

"Yes, of course, and I will. But do not concern yourself for me. I have rested all the time, in depths, in your silences. (I have rested while your face carried the reflection of strong torrents downstream – I have been with you at all of them – will you now walk in this coolness with me?)"

37

"Together?"

"Together."

"In silence?"

"In solitude."

"Shall we walk among the trees along the bank – smelling the elder's blossom, walking barefoot in sun-warmed grasses beyond the beach? And when the sun is lowered and the shadows creep over the water extinguishing the brilliants one by one, will we then return along the easy passage down the stream – with reddened day burnishing our faces, to the city and our friends, to the tall banks and the taller buildings – to the life that we have left for the space of an afternoon? Will we then float back over rapids, will we be able to say that we have loved, that we love?"

"Yes, we love, we love on an afternoon such as this."

Winter. The Claypath slopes upward, there is gravel underfoot. Low voices drift up to where a few lights remain among darkened windows.

"Now we walk with footsteps in uneven and hollowed echo. We move along the passage up to the hilltop. One rise is for Bede's College, two is for Hild's, one rise is for Bede . . ."

"Yes, and please stay. In winter all things are covered;

all things are disguised. Nothing is as it seems. This lamplight pierces the branches where once it burnished the leaves. Remember that the air is now cutting, is chilling to the skin."

"I remember when the air was heavy with blossom, was warm to the face."

"Yes! Remember that warmth. Think of winter's discord: of the moths no longer playing for the lamplight cutting crystalline paths through frozen branches. See, it touches my face but haloes yours."

"For me there will be the encounter by the bar, friendship's cadences and the warmth: your hand in mine. Feel it still, though I am heavy with winter teach me to love."

The wind waits for the two figures: a circle game played with the leaves of summer. The wind scurries among the white flakes and brown leaves at the top of the rise where they must pause. The lamplight stretches out the darkened forms on the ground – struggles to where the wind marks time.

"And I will now hope that I shall love you once more for the summer love bends, it fractures under winter's torment and the wind and the night (two figures: strange, fearsome even) collude with winter. Urgently, your feelings must wash over me for I feel that I withdraw."

"And so I will love you enough. Now that you tremble, afraid that you withdraw, I can breathe and happily be mistaken. My own cold image, for the two of us must be enough."

"It will, yes, if you wish it to be so."

And the girl was made glad. Thus a tremor is seen to pass along the banks of the river, and the faces – mobile, etched like the faces in a fire (the figures among the trees that resemble the trees) call – but not gladly nor yet out loud. They speak:

"WE WILL FOLLOW YOU NOW. FOLLOW FROM NOW ON."

The gusts admonish and the street lights flicker – perhaps a warning or a record of this passing. The hollow street sounds to a new set of footsteps and it rears up and away from the river at last. One rise is for Bede.

"WE WILL FOLLOW AS MISSHAPEN GROTESQUES AND WHITENED FACES. SO THAT YOU – STARTING AT STRANGE NOISES NOW AND AT TIMES IN THE NIGHT - WILL SEE THAT THE WIND IS DRIVEN HOWLING INTO YOUR DREAMS, THAT THE MOUNTAIN TOPS ARE SWATHED WITH MIST AND THAT WE, THE TRAVELLERS, THUS LASH OUTWARDS AT THE FINGER-BRANCHES, TWO COLD FACES, YOUR HANDS, AND WHAT YOU HAVE DARED TO HOPE FOR HEEDLESSLY."

The crowd ebbs and they move forward. Once silent, the city now flows: at this moment it menaces. As the young man winces from the pain that noise makes, he feels, perhaps, that perilous life has hardened to its point. But the girl is made desperate. She gestures towards flight.

"Quick! For we can yet escape! We can leave this concourse of the wind and the rain – the second rise – and across the bridge make for where safety lies."

And so begins their nightly odyssey: black, burning, their path is now endless, and over the fields and hills (with grey: an horizon slightly glimmering) they pass. And the corncrakes in the hedgerows, the small untrodden ditches: the night's small impression – is finally stilled. They flee, they are made silent, they are bright and now crystalline. On high they are able to look down, become insubstantial, and with cut, bleeding feet float free over the earth.

PART TWO

CHAPTER FIVE

But Samantha replied with her own tale and so gladdened the day. She spoke about the movement.

She was bright. Her smile was cheery so the sun shone hotly, it spread rapidly through the trees. For Samantha, her link with both university and Dunelm House – I can bring about an understanding: everyone then will be wise beyond belief – proved that not one single thing was wrong with the world. As a consequence, the zephyr blowing small ripples on the water was rightfully cold. The subtle chill was to be welcomed.

Her largesse included me. I would, she assured me, be able to feel a new spirit as I moved about the building. Samantha had noticed this herself at the moment of departure. It reminded her, she said, of the earliest days – which were days of high romance and the most severe of struggles.

"Oh! If you stay here tonight," she said, making the broadest of gestures, "it'll be romantic, it will be marvellous!"

At this she began describing the huge hall where people sat throughout the night, for Samantha had once stayed on, had once slept in the building and the impression it left was expansive; it now was blossoming.

"All that it was possible to see," Samantha began, " . . . were faces. For candles lit the hall and the huddled figures gathered round each one of them – islands of light – so that within each warm glow, smiling faces could be seen." Samantha then described the brilliance which at times lit up peoples' hair, the mellowness of everyone's eyes and the gentle kind of singing which rose up periodically from the crowds within the hall.

"Right into the far distance you could see these flickering points of light. So the walls seemed not to exist at all and the candles fused into a distant sea – and on this ocean, waves might then appear whenever faces were turned or other small gestures rapidly made.

"Many figures were huddled in sleep. For these apparently, duty dictated that they renew their energies – so they might give of their best to the movement on the day which was to follow. Others though, having a different calling, entertained one another and so bolstered the others' spirits. Their tales were of self-sacrifice and valour. They were filled with dedication and idealism.

"The gently flickering candles disappeared into the distance, so that only to those near the entrance would the hall have appeared like a room at all. Instead, the effect was of a camp in the open and the large number of fires was the multitude of candles, and people sat round these flickering flames. Or else the hall was like the ocean."

Samantha slept at the very centre of the gathering. This was more the focus than any real centre: "When one is adrift in a sea of lights," she said, "who can say where the centre might be?

"And the focus itself was a shifting though much more real experience. At moments throughout the night, tales from certain well-respected figures would draw large crowds and a shifting population of adherents would wander among the groups. They would then gather apocryphal tales and these, when re-told, would be suffused with the knowledge they had gained from other such heroes and so stories circulated and grew as well: they took on the colouring of the movement itself.

"The tales themselves could be moving. At one time some distinguished figure might choose to tell the story of an early helper; one who had, perhaps, narrowly missed giving service at the very beginning of the movement itself. Such early disappointment would be lifted perhaps by later inspiring activities. These deeds would perhaps have been performed, in spite of the most severe hardship and always, of course, in the interests of the greater whole. Early helpers in the movement, therefore, have possessed the most attractive of auras; they have always appeared simply suffused with enthusiasm.

"But early helpers are rarely seen. Such figures work so constantly that little relaxation is given them – their identities, as a consequence, are completely hidden. This is as it should be for they represent most fully the aims of the cause itself. Necessarily, then, they never admit to their involvement and because of this, the whole story cannot ever be known.

"Mind you," she said, "if you do stay, everything will be so much fun!" She squeezed my hand and she wrote out an introduction. On the note she spelt the word *Roger* and her concern was expressed in her gestures. She finished in this way: "I know you'll like him!" She let go of my hand.

At this she began describing the breakfast of the morning which followed her night in the building. Immediately, Samantha broke off and very graphically mimed the mutual feeding, the three vast plates, her own complete acceptance of these customs – and at this unattractive aspect of life within the building she began her discourse on the topic of sex.

"I know a lot is whispered about the promiscuity of those who stay overnight within these barricades. As far as rumours go, I am very probably one of the first ever to know.

"There are though, lots of people who flock to the

46

movement's side, and for them the interrogation rooms are perhaps a first step towards a hoped-for period of greater ease in sex. Such people, of course, are vetted very carefully indeed.

"This is just one more way in which the organization demonstrates its sensitivity. Like this it shows itself to think and act organically. It adapts to the opinions within and outside. In fact, by constantly monitoring the general mood and acting accordingly it retains its role as a true movement of . . . " She broke off and the light shone from the photographer's eyes and the hope and the love of Samantha fell lightly upon Roger and the gentle movement, and upon the others, these consorts of hers for that single glistening night.

She spoke again at last: "Do you like to hear about this work?"

"Yes, I do."

"All right, so I'll continue:

"It may be that you could eventually be of some help. Your mathematical aptitude could be put to good use and it would help in a number of different ways if you were to say – at least in the first instance – that you would like to work in the interpreting rooms."

"The interpreting rooms?"

"Where the flow diagrams are kept. With training you could help to interpret them . . ."

"Really?"

" . . . And the flow diagrams outline the policy of the movement. It would be key work . . . yes . . . but your manner would enable you to do it. You could succeed in this very unusual task."

We got up to move. "Shall we go there now?"

"Yes." So that nodding to each other we walked slowly across the towpath. We walked up the steep bank and into the shelter of the overhanging trees.

CHAPTER SIX

At this point Samantha looked about her strangely. Her eyes ranged about her as low willow branches caught in her hair. She spoke – and exceptionally some answer seemed to come: the bushes caught in the wind, leaves rustled, wavelets formed patterns and moved steadily by the bank. I turned my head – and her arms, her small hands waved, perhaps pointed. They were then raised to her mouth.

Samantha: "And now I see the figures in the trees – the whitened features, mobile – like the faces in a fire. Etched now in the willows by the river bank. The trees and the figures that resemble the trees – calling.

"But not for me."

The figures speak:

> *"FROM OUR POSITION BY THE RIVER WE ARE WELL PLACED TO SEE HE WHO HAS SPOKEN TO US, ENTERTAINING US, FOR A WHILE. WE, THE ORDINARY PEOPLE WHOM YOU PASS ON ANY STREET; WE, THE WHITENED FACES YOU TEND TO IGNORE HAVE ALLOWED HIM TO PASS AMONG US. WE THINK WE KNOW WHERE HE IS GOING.*

> *"GENERALLY WE PREFER TO PASS UNNOTICED AND USUALLY WE ACHIEVE THIS, BLENDING QUITE EFFECTIVELY. BLENDING WITH*

THE TREES IF YOU WALK BY THE RIVER, WITH THE WIND AND THE DRIVEN LEAVES IF YOU VENTURE UP THE CLAYPATH. NO ONE NOTICES US THERE.

"AT SUCH POINTS, TOO, YOU WILL DANCE. YOU WILL DANCE LIGHTLY WITH THE WIND – OR WITH SONOROUS STEPS INSIDE THE CATHEDRAL. TWISTING AND THEN FEINTING, YOU WILL SAY THAT NOTHING IS HAPPENING, THAT NOBODY RIDICULES YOU. WE LIKE IT THAT WAY."

The figures among themselves:

" . . . AND WHILE THIS DREAM LIES SOMEWHERE HIDDEN AND WHILE RESERVES WHICH WE FIND IMPORTANT RAPIDLY FAIL; WE CAN THEN BE ASSURED OF A NIGHT'S CERTAIN HARVEST."

The figures disappear.

Samantha: "Oh, I am unable to fathom the meaning of this dream! It is certain that these figures wait and would take some reward if they could. Certain, too, that they have wished to show themselves – and that they look towards you, the *dear one.*"

The wind then gusted and disturbed all the leaves.

CHAPTER SEVEN

Samantha turned to me once more. No recollection seemed to be present. The trees bent low; we made straight for Dunelm House and as we walked on we were joined by Reverend Ashley.

The priest spoke: "Are you going into the building?"

"Yes, it's the happiest place of all."

Reverend Ashley was out of breath. "I've come from the hospital: it was there we took Stephen." As the priest ran beside us he needed to talk of the event:

"The poor young man with the wound from the boat hook. Where his chest cavity was entered the lung tissue was exposed. He was torn and bleeding – even water flowed out.

"But we worked on him with determination – and the students held back the crowd, they cleaned up the wound and removed most of the mud and some of the water.

"Stephen was on the bank by the time that I arrived. However, as he drifted towards the weir, he had been cut; the flesh had been penetrated. The boat hook which was used on him – the hook sank right in.

"It happened like this:

"Stephen drifted and sharp objects in the river cut into his flesh – or else he was stabbed.

"At the weir he became trapped along with dead branches, refuse, the remains of the rowing eight.

"And a new boat went out with four strong rowers and another still stronger man – he was to pull Stephen to the shore.

"They fought against the current. The boat spun round – they were not strong enough.

"They broke through the entangling branches. Stephen's chest was severely pierced. Like this, he was towed eventually to the bank. As they did so, blood and brown river water came flowing out. He lay face down and they pressed very hard to empty the lungs.

"The doctor came. We listened to Stephen's whisper. Something final passed his lips.

"But Stephen *died* in this action – the crowd will know exactly who is to blame – and if the organization is not responsible then certainly there will be someone else – someone hiding now – someone who is.

"For Stephen's action was brave. What remains is my errand – to retrieve his file. Perhaps we can be companions for this part of the journey?"

And then – with some different intention in mind: "They tell me you were present at the very beginning of this organization?"

I protested vehemently, Samantha shook her head.

"Oh! But I've been assured you were!

"Surely it was you whom we saw at the student centre . . . yes, certainly . . . you are implicated very deeply."

I looked at the priest anxiously. Samantha showed a little pride.

"Yes," the priest continued. "Laura was there, Christopher, David too. Your first day in the university. You met them all there.

"And Ruth is within the barricades, and Theo too – and you, you were present at the very beginning!"

I could not remember – I was becoming confused with every moment. I didn't nod.

At precisely that moment, rapid paces were heard. At the same time, too, the whispering of voices.

I looked towards the priest. No more sounds could be heard but at the other end, the street was filling up. There were students standing at every one of the doors. Between each of the doorways a small figure was seen to race – and he questioned the inmates, each of whom nodded. Later they were to shake their heads, and only later still to point directly at me.

"There is one small passage, an escape, and a vennel on the corner." Reverend Ashley cried out. So the three of us ran quickly. Past two shop windows and an open doorway we flew.

There could be no mistake now. Our steps became more difficult – while running footfalls pursued. My companions urged me on; this was loyal and a little kind.

Through the town – streets somehow empty – empty streets because of sudden rain. We raced ahead. As we ran, the film on the cobbles, the speckles, made the passage slippery. We flew further ahead till, at the top of the path, we could see within the mist – a veil about a face – the cathedral, beckoning, not quite lifelessly. The priest turned from the scene.

Vennel faces appear not to have left me, and we look away from the mist. Samantha holds out her hand:

"There is a lot which is unsaid!"

My silence.

And we rush forward once more. From the top of the rise the way to the far side of the river is clear. We tumble down the bank.

While:

Staffs of light prod at the rock face; at drops forming, at glistening rivulets.

While there are low water sounds. Silences in between. And we stand leaning into the gulf as the rain percolates, it seeps through to the skin. The priest turns to me:

"Think of your own record."

Samantha looked at him: she could not agree with the suggestion of guilt.

"Laura was there?

"At the student centre. Yes?

"She befriended you?"

"Yes."

"And at the same time there were Roger and David, Christopher . . . more people than you might think. How did you find the company?"

"It was friendly, unpleasant. I rushed out of the building very, very soon."

"Yet there was important work going on. You sensed the disharmony yet you failed to discover where friends might then lead you.

"It is others who are searching for you now!"

(Just as the rock on which I alight – dewed, moss-covered – moves. This great weight slips, grinds small crystals, and the leaves of grass bend: they are trampled under my feet.)

We run on ahead. Reverend Ashley: "That is the way!"

We descend through the woods. Voices echo through the trees' shade – I look into vacant eyes, cold eyes, and those which pass with fear for my emptiness.

Samantha: "Look! There's the building! Where the sun slips through the mist on the far side of the river!"

We rush past small houses which nestle at the weir: a rapid, tortuous, a determined pace. We come close to the river and the river sounds: the insignificant pulses on a waking day. (They are charged with the minutes, the seconds between the ticking of the clock. Faces and voices tumble and rise. As we take the river path they fade perceptibly. For a minute I can see the structure and then no more. A leaf full of the rain's sparkling, the sun's pallor, drifts past fluidly: I grasp for it. My fingers rapidly close.)

We move on: For a moment I can hold the pattern and then no more. I am left staring up at a burnished sun, a strange, indistinct and changing sun. One that cannot be recognized and is unworthy of trust.

We rush down the bankside. Over our heads rain falls too, striking the canopy – green, this is now becoming yellowed. And the ripples of the water falling – down the surface of the barks – still the air, my fears. Damp smells arise. We hasten ahead to make what progress we may.

The far bank is radiant. The sun is on the leaves, it even sparkles on the trees. The circle game following us – above each of our heads – is plainly visible in the light, the vivid sunlight – which pours onto the far bank. (As the wind gusts, the trees shift and circling, sway – as I have seen cornfields sway – and beneath these trees, too, there will be the drip of bright water.)

Dunelm House is seen to rise, it towers above us all. The sun is shining for just this spot on the bank. While mist from the warmed leaves swirls slightly, it is caught in the winds. The sun brings out rainbow lights. All paths to the parapets are obscured in green leaves.

Water drips and insects dart, they hum now right out loud. The sun moves across the face of the building. The windows, proclaiming the movement, glare, dazzle: they shine quite brilliantly. The whiteness which thus moves so suddenly is the light from the sun, it is the fine reflection of the clear day of the sun. It is the best hope, the breath and warmth, the comfort of the sun. Salvation, refuge, true destiny. My destiny too – or kind souls must be wrong.

Samantha holds her hand out, she has fallen some way behind. Running so that we must leap across obstacles –

sinking some way into soft turf with each of our paces – Samantha now needs our help. The priest reaches out, she is helped over logs. Samantha and the priest are loyal and kind indeed: these angry pursuers need reach only me.

The walls rise above us. The sky is blotted out. The chase is coming closer I can hear angry cries. My limbs move slowly: I am caught by the small branches, each and every thorn.

The first of my pursuers breaks through the undergrowth. The three of us rush further up, nearer to the walls. And cries can now be heard from the glistening parapets – which drift majestically above us.

The wind which is now drying the leaves, shakes them so that small droplets – shining – fall the eighty or so feet. They twist and arc spiralling. They descend and they catch at the walls. They fly over our heads and shoot glisteningly in an infinite fall.

For seconds they sink and the sunlight is caught in them. It is there changed by them and their colours are reflected on the walls. Samantha struggles. Finally there is a stream.

The stream falls down the banks and it enters the river. At times the water tumbles: a broken, jagged waterfall. Now it is a barrier and we must cross the turbulent water. The followers must do so too. The priest finds large stepping stones. He hops lightly across: one, two, three. The current and his foot's pressure loosen all of them but one. As I approach the stream I must wade in some way. And beyond, over shrubs and thickets, over the bluff (coal seams can be seen: four feet thick, the northern Durham coalfield), over the summit of this rise – the steps of Dunelm House, the balustrade and the cordon and the crowds.

We struggle over the top. Through the oak doors which are now visible, gesturing figures can be seen. Were the pace less rapid we might stop now and decide who could possibly be there.

Christopher's face is partly visible. He at least is welcoming. And then a rapid change: the figures still indistinguishable – their gestures suddenly show a sublime indifference. They are not now encouraging: the mistake has been a fault, and a grievous one.

I now understand I have not been able to recognize even one of the students, townspeople, antagonists who are following us. Towards the bridge, the area of Kingsgate is full of small figures. These rush, some of them backwards - they are encouraging the others – and so a large host seems intent upon some resolution, for they shout, breathe, wave and gesture instructions. They cause their vast number to swell. They mass now in hundreds and they fill every part of the bridge.

Some of the people are now crossing the stream. For the following throng all difficulties must be slight. Groups of people flood from the colleges towards the bridge. For a few, their cries are not yet angry, while others bear every degree of agitation so that at once the crowd is cheerful, overbearing or caught up in festering anger.

For the three of us, therefore, it is a fearful sight. We run towards the steps. The first to reach the wall of the building and to push through the enveloping crowds is the priest. He does so forcefully – he is thinking clearly of us two – and when Samantha and I follow, the crowds shift, they fall back apace and on passing into the throng I am forced into acts of obeisance hardly at all.

Reverend Ashley reaches the doorway and tries to speak – jeers surround us, Christopher has gestured to the crowd. Samantha who is to be welcomed enters into the building as the cordon opens wide. With breath in small bursts I cry out; the oak door opens partially, it closes promptly behind me – and the broad sweep of bystanders closes up. People hammer on the door. Police push them away.

Christopher is accompanied by three interrogators and he is

quick to point them out to me. Reverend Ashley, once inside the cordon, immediately sets about his tasks as if the place itself held no terrors for him and as if he had never expressed to me the slightest degree of reserve. Straightaway, he states his several objectives, makes his claim upon privilege; asks for and receives some temporary note, a talisman that will enable him to pursue enquiries in some remote corner; makes clear the limit of his intended stay - and is led away with for him the promise that "exceptions will be made".

Samantha looks about her rather awkwardly. "I'll show you the way," she ventures and involves us all in her uncertainty. Samantha is welcomed: "Friend – your advice and your help have been greatly missed." But in the air of impermanence which attaches to this entranceway, the photographer realizes decisions are to be made and that from this point on, paths might now diverge.

Something natural seems to be taking place. That the priest is made confident by his mission and by the reception he has received; that Samantha, her position already one of glorious ambivalence is set in a rare vibration; that I am caught by the elbow and ushered onwards and inwards; that David is no longer present but that Christopher is; that the three interrogators are now sent to control and instruct us; that the crowd is shouting outside while within the building all is quiet and calm – all this is natural indeed – and fearsome and strange, too, are the folds that the movement now encloses me in.

Samantha's parting gestures – her caring glances – included, surreptitiously, a brief look at the photographs she had taken of me; several departing kisses, and at length, her recapitulation of the aims and beauty of life within the organisation. She reminded me of the zealots; encouraged me in my search for assistance from above – she pressed forward Roger's name – and spoke again of the lightening effect of days and nights spent in this rarefied company.

All these points caught her imagination exceptionally: she spoke of ways of obtaining help from established individuals - and so filled several minutes of the assembled company's time.

At this the interrogators showed some irritation – which Samantha dismissed as lewdness – but finally after a great length of time they began to gesture that they had heard all this before; that they had been aware of our discussion outside the barricades, and that nothing that Samantha was presently saying could be new to them at all.

The priest announced that pacification of the crowd outside would now be of the utmost importance to him, whereupon the interrogators – all three of them – turned, stared, and thus impressed their joint presence upon me.

Their gestures became more and more agitated. It seemed they were definitely making their minds up to say something. It was obvious they felt that one of their number would have to speak to me, it was now merely a matter of settling who it should be. Each of them was indicating that he felt this or that had to be said, each was desperately trying to convince his fellows of the need for his particular point to be brought to my attention, but equally, each protagonist felt his own point would have to be made not by himself, but by one of his fellows. The game seemed endless.

I turned rather wearily towards the nearest one.

"What do you want to say?"

"We feel we must caution you."

The words were whispered, but still a number of people in the nearby corridor turned to listen.

"We must warn you against this seemingly naïve approach. While we have been here listening we have noticed that our friend Samantha has taken a far too simplified view of our aims. We are saddened by this apparent lack of understanding, especially from someone who is reckoned to be among the friends of our movement. This lapse becomes only comprehensible if we assume that our friend is suffering from a temporary lack of judgement due, we feel, to the close attachment she appears to have formed with yourself.

"We disregard the fact that she dismisses our interest in this side of her affairs as merely licentious – we are used to such barbs – as is everyone within the organization. But we are concerned that some faulty opinions which she has voiced might actually at some time be adopted by you. In your present state this might not be too damaging – here we must think only of the movement – nevertheless, it may happen that one day you will be one of our number and it is then that the harm will begin to show.

"Up to this point we commend you on your good sense – you appear to have taken a more realistic approach to your prospects than friend Samantha has encouraged you to do. We even commend the enthusiasm with which she has described certain aspects of our life within Dunelm House, but we must, as I say, make our view felt.

"We applaud your sensible attitude and warn against any change you might be considering. We also applaud your zeal, for although we do not approve of the idea of seeking favour from higher individuals, nevertheless, we feel the proper way to view your efforts is to assume that you wish to locate certain persons so that, perhaps, a point or two might be clarified.

"In this light we applaud your efforts. For anything which helps an interrogator advances the movement by just that amount. We wish you all speed."

The speaker stopped. A silence fell upon the company. Christopher, standing in the background, did not seem to want to come any further forward and Samantha, unable to hear everything that was being said, had taken to ushering people into her booth and so had resumed her work instead. Only I listened attentively. After a time, one of the other interrogators, becoming restless, indicated that he too would like to speak and so he addressed us all:

"Actually," he began, "what my friend says is true. It really is foolish to imagine you could work in the interpreting rooms. In fact, we would be failing in our duty if we didn't point out that such places which do fall vacant are filled – as a matter of course – from among established helpers. It would be misleading if it were once suggested a mere newcomer could ever be admitted to them, and so I suggest the best place for you to look for your friends is in the library instead, where records of all activities are kept – and not merely the recent admissions. The suggestion is so elementary I am amazed at Christopher for not thinking of it himself."

At this, the conversation died away. I tried several times to engage the interrogators in further discussion but apart from a few limited signs – these were drawn on my hand, with collective energy they gripped my index finger, clutching it hotly, and drew and redrew moist symbols on my palm – apart from these excesses, the three interrogators now took on a strange and immense calm. In progressive stages they became immobile like the sphinx.

Christopher, the painter, now led the way. Without turning round to see if he was being overheard, Christopher explained that the interrogators were only there to observe; that they might, on occasion, proffer information, but that this information would only be given after extensive joint consultation and thereafter it would be impossible for any of them to take further part in anyone's affairs.

On this occasion, Christopher said, the interrogators had really been exceptionally helpful. He, himself, would never have thought of the library, especially since, except for the early days, he had never been invited within.

"But then it'll be different for you," he said, and went on to explain that someone like myself – of imposing appearance –

could end up quite naturally as an upright member of some very high level group indeed. He thought suddenly of the first time I saw him inside the building: "The cubicles are quite finished now," he said, and thus unerringly completed my private thoughts for me.

We set off together in the direction of the library – Samantha now was exempted, advised that the strain of entering the area of such excellence was better avoided – and as we walked on I looked about me trying to recognize remaining signs of the building's earlier use. The present transformation was really quite complete. No signs had been allowed to remain, and the spots marking former notice boards were white and painted over. Samantha pointed to these just as her camera whirred and clicked furiously and thus she took her memento of our five departing backs.

"She's more trouble than she's worth," said Christopher, trying to avoid her panchromatic attention, and he explained that for someone wanted by a screaming crowd outside and presently engaged upon a desperate search, photographic mis-evidence was the last thing that was required. I ignored this criticism and thought quietly of Ruth.

"You won't recognize where we are!" He volunteered quite cheerfully – for all the earlier life had gone. The corridor was recently painted, now it was strange.

We ducked behind the place of a former notice board. In the shadow there now appeared the longest corridor yet encountered – and this corridor was clean, it was tidy. In this way the finer lights among the helpers had supported each other - and their embrace had grown, it had increased to become, quite unexpectedly, the essence of the organization. And the movement would thus gather joyfully about us, it would become like the sun. To the accompaniment of Christopher's silent nodding and the interrogators' agreement – they, all four of them, read accurately my silent thoughts.

"Don't worry too much about the corridor," someone's kind voice said gently from behind. "If it doesn't seem to fit with the building's former appearance it could be that your memory is faulty. Or else, perhaps genuine and important changes have already taken place." In this way I was unexpectedly reassured so I immediately stopped wondering at all and settled to looking about me. I glanced up and down the corridor catching sight of faces once or twice from behind partially opened doors. I looked for them, fixed their gaze occasionally, and shuddered at each such strange, too close meeting. The doors shut peremptorily, their eyes never blinked.

"It isn't far to the library," one of the interrogators said and the cheerfulness of the tone was endorsed by the others who nodded their heads with a precision which startled even Christopher and seemed almost mechanical. Only the painter seemed apprehensive about our approach. It occurred to me that the exhilaration of the interrogators might prove to be a warning for Christopher; that in the regions where we were approaching only certain personnel might find themselves welcome. (I felt satisfied of my own acceptability: Christopher had assured me of this. A fresh burst of laughter confirmed just this point.)

The corridor walls were of exposed plaster. Everywhere they showed the grain from the original wooden shuttering. It was as if the walls were trying to be both concrete and wooden – though the imprint of scaffolding confounded both these aspirations. And the doors on either side were painted brown or else green. Each hue was different but varied between these two limiting colours. Christopher took some pride in pointing out the subtleties of the shading – surely a painter's pride – though his choice of green and brown owed more to the gravedigger's eye, reflecting as it did the green of the turf and the brown of the Highgate soil. I looked with apprehension for the black and cream cheese white that I half expected.

Christopher all unknowing did not share my misgivings.

Christopher's manner changed perceptibly. Instead of the painter who was confident enough to suggest, actually suggest, an interpreting room as a place where Theo and Peter might be found, he now appeared smaller than usual and just a little frightened. Perhaps before, when he came along this corridor in his painter's role, perhaps then he had the companionship of David to bolster his spirits. Certainly on that occasion his work had not suffered unduly and although some of the doors showed brown streaks among the overall green, nevertheless, the slabs of colour *were* rectangular and only in places did his brush slip so that the grey of the plaster became reminded of the Durham grass and the earth outside.

Now the interrogators were showing signs of unease. Their discomfort showed itself as indecision among their number. Instead of following my steps with a quite deliberate unison, they now rushed backward and forth so that sometimes one might actually run ahead of me – anticipating my steps as it were – but always paying great attention to the paintwork and afterwards commenting on the degree of agitation which the brush strokes had shown – so throwing the author of these strokes into greater and greater confusion.

Yet Christopher's confusion might be due to other causes. Like me, he was alone and surely the object, too, of the interrogators' attention. Equally, Christopher without his companion might fail to understand the strictures that apparently were to follow – for David, in spite of a certain maliciousness, was surely Christopher's comrade and guide. And so, while my mind was fixed upon Theo, Peter, my file and Ruth; Christopher's moans were for his lost past and early splendour: the trust, indeed, and hope, the love of dear friends.

But here, at least, the painter's work was supreme. Nothing of the grey shuttering-faced walls detracted from the painterly efforts which now resembled not so much doors in a corridor but the work – displayed in fine galleries – of bright intimate art. But these artists clearly had progressed beyond the rectangular. Their work, no longer limited to the regions of the doors, set out in streaks of green and brown to march across a canvas which resembled the outline of the doors only in the barest of details.

Instead of such constraint these strident browns and greens, unmixed and existing in whorls as well as drips, covered large areas of wall, often missing their doors – by intention – so completely that the rectangles remained as rough aftershadows – faint recollections – ignored perhaps by the painter in brown and his friend who preferred green.

Christopher was not able to see, however. Christopher's time for painting doors with or without his companion was far from his mind. And if anyone were to ask him about the curious abstracted quality he brought to his work, then that person would receive no reply that was intelligible or else no reply at all, because Christopher by now had sunk right down to his knees. Christopher trembled. With small sobs and a coughing of blood he mouthed meaningless words and his eyes stared down the corridor which still stretched perhaps twenty yards ahead. He stared at rows and rows of still unpainted doors to the point where we could see every last effort finally had been given up. A dozen feet from this point, Christopher now lay prostrate and – pleading fitfully to be left alone – he gestured; he asked to be omitted from the reckoning and asked, too, to be excused from further advance into the region of the library.

The interrogators showed no willingness to answer. They too were in an agitated state. They did not notice, as I had, that Christopher's blood came from a cut in his tongue – self-mutilation during agitated mouthings – especially as these interrogators were now rushing some little way ahead of us, were peering round the bend in the corridor and then returning, often, to huddle together amid their loud whisperings.

It was obvious to me that if we were ever to reach the library I would have to lead the way. Although I didn't know its whereabouts, I indicated to the others that very probably the only way was forward, especially since that section of the corridor which lay behind us now appeared completely unrecognisable.

Everyone nodded. Something in the look exchanged by the interrogators encouraged me, they imitated in a frightened way my every gesture. Soon, after passing the last limiting trace of paint - the end of David's previous incursion – we began to hear noises; so henceforth our steps were then guided whenever a decision was forced upon us by a junction or a dividing passageway.

The noises were of rustling paper and a host of low murmurings. It was as if a thousand monks were reciting their breviaries: each then would seem to continue with low sounds so as not to disturb the others.

By the time we entered that part of the corridor where the library door was situated we could see it actually stood half-open and as a consequence soft sounds were now escaping, even though we were not as yet able to see what lay within. I was swept up in the hysteria which affected Christopher and David too, on a previous occasion. I was rapidly becoming like the interrogators. I became caught up in their frenetic corridor dance. I rushed forward and back so that at times I saw a half-open door and a bright light within, and at other times traces of the partially painted walls: greens and browns and the red of Christopher's saliva.

Nowhere were my fellows to be found. Somehow they had tired of the dance, or if not this, then they had certainly declined to take part, now that I too was involved. Obviously my inclusion had made it invalid or at least unnecessary for them to continue. I felt, however, that this dance was the natural consequence of all of my actions so far. The dance, the hysteria, might have been designed for me, and so it was that suffused in a polychrome terror I blundered into the partially opened doorway, into the light and into the library itself.

The light was blinding. Looking about me, horribly exposed, I saw that to the far distance every available corner, every horizontal surface carried fluorescent desk lamps, adjustable reading lamps, brilliant flood lamps and overhead penetrating spotlights. Clusters of lamps nestled around – on specially constructed trolleys – and the tangled flexes from this host of mobiles littered the floor. This entangling carpet was in places inches thick.

Little groups of people sat, their faces brilliantly lit, and indeed, as I entered the library, attendants rushed about adjusting lamps – all those that were available – so that my face like everyone else's was completely bathed in enveloping light.

In each of the groups only one person would speak at any single time. Generally, the monologue was accompanied by intricate hand signals and only occasionally did the mentor resort to audible speech. Nevertheless, so vast was the number of these groups that merely by their occasional whisperings was a deadening sibilance made to fill the air.

Even so, notes did pass sometimes between these librarians. On occasion, when a particular member was having special difficulty – perhaps a word, more rarely a whole phrase – then indeed the dumb-show, the language of gestures was abandoned and so the sense of the idea was written down, at other times it was whispered. And such was the number of the working groups of librarians that these murmurings became truly vast and the rustling of the rare paper notes taken at large became the ocean's roar. It could have been heard for miles.

Only a few eyes turned upon my entry and then only momentarily so. For the most part each worker had eyes only for those fellows within his group. Staring into the distance where the nested lamps appeared as no more than specks of light – beyond that disappearing completely – I felt suddenly the depth of my isolation. I felt fully for my companions – lacking in courage – who had so failed to penetrate even beyond certain of the outer reaches. I wondered how the organization obtained the power for so many, many lights; and I wondered where within the building my own courage, too, might be expected to fail.

And I was right. Something told me that this bravery was not nearly enough so that sensing the thought's exterior nature I turned to see who could possibly be putting such ideas into my head.

The eyes behind me – wide, knowing, tempered unfathomably - were green. They were the wide, sweet, gentle eyes that I loved. Even though a photographer's art had blinded me with magnesium bulbs, bulbs whose brilliance had turned my head so that not quite official clothes fell then in a heap upon a strange floor, even then the green eyes had smiled for me and reminded the whole world that they waited not quite out of sight, not quite out of my memory, for they waited then, poisonously, with a tender knowledge of me.

I walked forward.

The glancing priest began saying prayers – amplified and to a congregation of angry parishioners – for me.

Doubts arise and the doctor's notes and the recorded faults – the long, lingering miasma – all are now weighing heavily. Heavily. And the grave-digger's shovel throws each massive sod. Heavy. A long, hollow, rattling fall. A hundred faces are swept silently aside and the doubting and the questions bloom as before.

Ruth: "They've begun chanting for you!"

And the anger is mounting with every minute. It rears itself up, bears me up; dashes me against the rocky adventure, the grey, shuttering-edged walls of Dunelm House.

Outside a few had made a start on their prayers. They prayed

67

for those in limbo, lost souls and the erring steps of this lost soul. They prayed finally and they called upon the God of the twisting gaze – the circling dance – to look after his own. They prayed with a desperation and they prayed for Stephen, his killer's true repentance, and they were thinking kindly and gently and even beautifully of me.

"But you're here!" And I grasped Ruth's hand, holding it, sliding it through terror-warmed palms. Ruth, truly graceful, was flooded in the light of so many adjustably attentive lights that this became a caressing time, a moment of glistening, iridescent embrace.

Rare warmth, happiness. And all the time the eyes were staring – and the gestures, difficult words, notes and messages rose in flight suddenly: they centred upon Ruth. And Ruth, in some part of the library sat lightly on a desk, and the blonde curls and the green eyes suddenly became the very thing that was needed. The library of shining light had waited longingly for this.

A detached voice: "If you have business in the library you must show evidence of it to the attendant seated some way to your left."

But the flight of librarians; bright, lightened, most delicate souls, responded to this beauty and vibrated sympathetically. To Ruth and my vision of her white light, this unreason, they palpitated monstrously. The air was charged sparklingly with a thousand rounded gestures.

I reached for Ruth's other hand. To the far ends (the lights glistened there, no longer distinguishable as points of light – in the far distance they merged beautifully into the whitest of nebulae); at the far ends gestures arose: anger, insistence and petulance, close possession. And thus were sent out tremors, undulations, wild, odd gesticulations so that throughout this gilded sea, the waves lit upon every one of the light-filled librarians.

Their anger was for me. Those nearest made their gestures in my direction. They felt clearly that the onus of remonstrating with me – for labour interrupted – was most heavily theirs.

"That is true," the speaker said. "But it has to be admitted that those closest to you are the ones who have been inconvenienced most."

I walked over to the desk. "We have a record of your interview with friend Laura in the interrogation rooms." Ruth, as interpreter, was whispering in my ear. I glanced again towards her but the assistant drew my attention. His grimace was made brilliant, was made fearsome – for a battery of lamps picked out every line of his face. He was shown gesticulating in dazzling relief. Had I been as good as Ruth at following his mime I would have found the brightness of the lighting very useful indeed.

"It is not normal," Ruth and the clerk were most anxious to insist, "for a newcomer to penetrate this far into the building. Normally the very nature of the organization makes it impossible for anyone – newcomer, early helper – to stray beyond his allotted locale."

Ruth indicated that the clerk should repeat this final word; the doubt once removed, they both immediately continued. The clerk's arms were flashing quite forcefully now. Five fingers represented the vowels, but apart from this, gestures involving not just the arms, but the face and body as well – those delicate and varied forms – impressed emotional overtones. The communication grew in subtlety minute by minute; it was a delicate and fluid language of its own. And Ruth was there to assist. She was able to help because my attention was especially captivated, it was seized by tortured faces appearing suddenly from the corridor – appearing from behind the half-opened door and briefly so, to disappear silently and completely and unhappily once more.

There seemed so little time for Ruth and me to say everything we needed to. All around eyes pressed me to spare the endeavour's time, to avoid the irrelevant or confusing statement: to give a total attention to the dutiful clerk, and Ruth, brightest star of the library of shining light; Ruth, blossoming, grew in strength as she interpreted for me, she willingly sped things along: "Anything at all to the help the dear, dear boy!"

And the clerk replied with harshness and all the venom of suppressed nightmares so that Ruth in the sweetest tones whispers:

"What is the purpose, darling, of your visit to the library?"

So I reply abruptly, speaking of Theo and Peter:

"There are records, the interrogating rooms will have sent mine on. Perhaps Theo and Peter will tell me where they are – if they don't work in the library already that is.

"Ruth, there is a secret!"

The clerk paused and Ruth paused too and the staggered silences spread outwards – for no apparent reason at all. And the mimed conversations halted and the ripples of disturbance spread out, and I did indeed feel people's hard eyes begin focusing on me.

The reply was abrupt. Simply: my search was an improper one, no answer would be possible. Something like a laugh sounded behind me and I thought for a moment that Christopher might have made it. The painter, however, had not come even near to the library. In spite of this I thought bitterly about him: he had first suggested that Theo and Peter might be in the interpreting rooms, he, therefore, was responsible for compromising me from the start.

"But why?" I demanded, becoming suddenly angered by the silence and the whole contrivance of mime, brilliant lighting and unanswerable questions.

But the reply when it did come took me no nearer to the truth. "We will not be able to answer the question, though, rest assured you will not remain in doubt for long. It is in the nature of the library that your question will be rendered unnecessary and isn't that the same as having an answer?"

There seemed no way of replying to this so I turned resignedly. Thoughtfully I contemplated the shining beauty in front of me. I gazed longingly and for a great space of time and fixedly at Ruth.

CHAPTER EIGHT

Ruth turned to me.

"If we try very hard we can probably find ourselves alone."

But the mere wish would not bring the massy walls of the building down nor cause the clerks, the groups of librarians, to disappear. Fading from the extremities first, what would then be left would be a certain disembodiment – a sense of presence.

But by simply taking the few steps to an alcove – at one time a broom-cupboard – we were able to shut off all the brightly lit stares and the murmurings which surged softly backward once my offending presence had been removed.

In an excess of the language of gestures my hands roamed and they sought for pleasure among the fine lace and Ruth's intimate clothes, "Will there be some future for us?" I asked, and Ruth replied:

"Silly! Of course there won't! But perhaps I can answer your question for you – at least in part."

We tumbled to the floor. This floor became sprinkled with the clothes that had swathed Ruth, had hidden her privately for just this moment.

"Yes, just for you," she said, ignoring the knocking on the door outside.

"Let's lie here and you can tell me gently what has happened." Had there been an aftertaste; how long had she been waiting in the library for me? Had word of the photographer's wiles reached her ears? I began to regret every moment of dalliance: there was no comparison, nor could there ever be.

Suddenly, the familiar world – affairs were well regulated, there was an understandable rationale – rushed forcefully back. Ruth would not remove my questions. She would move gently among my fears and at the end, while she caressed my hair, she would dispel them, answering freely and frankly so that my questions would not then disappear, like myself, in a surrogate death. She began at once:

"I was lost without you. I heard that you had walked away from the confusion at the river." She then added forcefully: "Stephen is dead, you know. You do realize that? When you followed that unknown figure and left us all to fend for ourselves it seemed to us you were abandoning everyone. You looked guilty, in that moment people found it easy to believe anything of you. You were being blamed before you got anywhere near Dunelm House."

"But it was for you!" I protested, thinking of my file. A file that it was necessary to keep permanently closed, a file written in part in a neat medical hand; a file that recorded an interview in which Ruth, like myself, was laid devastatingly bare: a secret Ruth, certainly a Ruth to be kept hidden from friends and acquaintances, from the movement, from herself, and especially from me.

And I continued to protest: "Everything was for you. Everything. When I waded into the water and dived toward Stephen – just a patch of green – that was for you; even my presence here. Everything – for you!"

At this Ruth smiled. The gratitude she showed seemed inadequate in the extreme. "If only you'd realize how far things have gone since then," she said, suddenly breaking off to look out through the chink in the door once more.

"What do you mean?"

"Well, the whole thing's suspended. Police are everywhere. The whole university has completely stopped. And so dear Simon . . ." She waved her hand and in doing so showed exactly why my efforts had been wasted. She turned her head suddenly to look impatiently away.

I looked toward Ruth desperately.

"Well, is it so very surprising, Simon, is it? Just think what has happened so far. By immense effort the movement is set up but no sooner has this happened than there is a revolt among the students and the police are called in. Everyone waits for the Vice-Chancellor's initiative." I thought of that initiative. I thought of Samantha and her two roles – Shire Hall and Dunelm House.

"And then there's an incident.

"From among the students, a rowing eight blithely rows past Dunelm House and the helpers inside react with missiles, rubbish and a volley of fire hoses.

"Trivial – except that Stephen got killed.

"And so with nothing to go on they thought of you. You, who had arrived at just the right time: you were certainly in the water when he was mysteriously killed.

"And finally, when you suddenly left the scene in the company of that odd character and disappeared into Dunelm House it began to look very sinister indeed.

"Simon, tell me, have you really sought refuge here?"

"I wanted to find my file," I replied rather lamely. "But before that I have to find Peter and Theo."

Ruth threw up her hands: "There's a crowd outside and it's waiting for you to come out. There isn't a suspect yet, but still, it's your name that is being chanted outside by the crowd!"

Ruth immediately began leafing through her diary. She

74

allowed me to see the pages but the writing itself was hard to make out.

She lightly tossed her head to look at me directly for just a moment before looking down again petulantly.

"What am I going to do?" I cried.

But Ruth did not have to answer the question because the hammering on the door began again. Relief and something alien passed across her eyes.

"Don't ask me questions like that," she said. "Can't you see I want to be happy?" And then with more of the hammering she turned away from me.

Ruth could not see who was making the noise and was trying to get in. Giggling, she turned herself slowly, displaying herself more fully – and I saw that the fevered eyes outside had found a crack through which to observe her – so that she said: "Oh, Peter and Theo! They're in the interpreting rooms – but I shouldn't have said that should I?"

"Where?" I said, but Ruth just looked down and leafed through a list of boys' names she had in her diary: she checked this lunch date with that evening one and so planned a social life which would surely make her happy indeed. (I felt the anger of my love, my lust, and I felt just the beginning of a fear for my life.)

But Ruth was in communion with the eyes that were outside – a certain diminished consciousness - so that Ruth, the toast of Dunelm House; Ruth, star of all the university and queen of the library of shining light; Ruth, singular, magnificent and unchallenged; Ruth, the centre of my devotion became in rapid, progressive steps and with quiet deliberation, Ruth, the lust-object of an army of librarians and interrogators . . .

"And guards, too! Don't forget the guards!" Ruth shuddered with delight: she moved even me.

"So Theo and Peter are not here in the library then?"

"Well, actually they are more in the interpreting rooms than in the library."

Surely, I thought, she must have meant more *often* in the interpreting rooms. But at this her eyes became angered and her pout became provocative.

I thought of Ruth's happiness.

"Ruth, let me give you your happiness!" But the pout never left her lips, she leant back while I suffused that pout with what passes for happiness and I brought forth pleasure – a moan, a cry of delight, sweet ecstasy. The ecstasy was for my body, it was not for me. Throughout, Ruth's eyes were fixed steadily on the crack in the door: it was a cold completion in which I was privileged to be included.

Look! Removed and distant essence of manhood. It is I who console, I who excite and penetrate. It is I who love while you, the surrogate man have only your eyes! Suddenly we separated, I looked directly at Ruth:

"Will you take me to them then?" And Ruth, breathing hard, stopped. She turned over briefly, she smiled.

"Why do you want to see them? They're here in the library."

"But – the interpreting rooms . . . ?" And Ruth stilled me with a sudden tenderness, a touch:

"It is better this way. The interpreting rooms would be a long way for you." I motioned to interrupt her. "But only because you would lose your way. There is every possibility that you would find them eventually. Especially since, in some way, too, I have been there myself.

"For me there was a guide."

"Roger?"

"Yes. He made the way easy. . ." The hammering began again. Ruth raised her voice: ". . . So I'm going to tell you all I know about the interpreting rooms themselves."

The door banged once more. Ruth raised her hands aloft. With neat and feminine gestures she modelled the movement. Regions which were familiar occurred in some of her hand movements and flashing between these were certain others indicating the figures that were dearest to me.

"The rooms are actually very small," Ruth motioned first, "though the whole complex is so vast it now fills out the Great Hall. After the movement was first established, the hall was partitioned off and the maze of little rooms results. In each room flow charts are constantly interpreted.

"But don't imagine these are in any way like the interrogation cubicles. The interpreting rooms were established much earlier and there has thus been sufficient time for the work to be properly finished off.

"When one is in one of these rooms it is quite impossible to know if it is near the centre of the complex or close to the periphery. Certainly the work has been done so well that none of the earlier building is visible at all.

"Each room is square and has a door to each wall. Some of the doors will connect to the perimeter by means of long, angled corridors, others of course, communicate directly to adjacent rooms. The corridors are essential otherwise one would have to pass through each of the outer rooms on the way to the centre.

"Even so, there is a tremendous amount of coming and going. Interpreters have to make long excursions through dozens of rooms just to get one point clarified. It is because of this confusion that the organization of the library has now been made so good: the problems of the interpreting rooms could not be solved without dismantling the whole structure, but with the new region of the library, things could be very different indeed. The first thing was the ban on talking. Every library that I have known demands some degree of silence."

"Nevertheless," I thought, "it is a large step from that to the elaborate structure of dumb-show used throughout the movement and only particularly in the library of shining light."

"No, it's not!" Ruth said instantly, once more knowing my

feelings completely. "Perhaps if you could understand our language of gestures then . . ." But she didn't finish the sentence.

"Simon," she said, "don't you think that inside here you're somehow out of place?"

"And you're not?"

"No, I'm not."

I stammered. The banging which had allowed Ruth's words, her affirmation, to resound, to brighten the day, recommenced – now that I was speaking – and my confidence fled. In her eyes I could see that it was better to agree.

"The interrogators warned me I would not reach the interpreting rooms at all . . ." but the hammering interrupted me again. Ruth, though, took so little notice that it was as if she hadn't heard – this, apparently, was the way the brilliant librarians were at that time conducting their work.

"You haven't understood much have you?" I made no reply but hoped in my inordinate struggle that Ruth would go on with her explanation. She did so at last: she described the flow diagrams.

"I was invited," Ruth said, ". . . and this was in spite of Roger's insistence, by some people – the most exceptional individuals – to think along certain special lines. And this intense meditation brought with it a certain awareness. The vision was vivid and represents an aspect of the truth that is certainly closer to the spirit of *cause* than anything yet described. Indeed, I have several people's word for this: when awakened from my dream they gathered round attentively, those who had had some slight dealing with the interpreters agreed that the exposition was enlightening."

I saw at once one more reason for Ruth's eminence.

"In my vision, as I walked through the doors I saw the interpreting rooms – and the people inside were uplifted by their fine labour. As they gathered attentively – here and there they would crowd round a table – their gestures would show the elation brought about by their work and they would pore over one chart and at the same time leave the others completely bare.

"And I saw quite clearly that the charts bore a system of whorls; that these dark lines were complex and they ran in their convolutions over every inch of the paper's surface. And the interpreters' gestures became excited, they held up their hands and what was clearly being discussed were the activities going on at that moment within the movement. Some of these – the daily routines – formed closed loops (the cleaners' own lines returned time and time again) so that for people represented in this way, their days varied little and each night was spent in the very same place.

"But what seemed to take up most of the interpreters' time were the really subtle patterns: the projects – involving aggregations of workers (to each an individual line) – which in this way took on the form of clusters, or else of bundles. These lines twisted and marched across the charts thus the course of the venture was marked in the progression of these lines so that to each loyal worker and at each moment of the day there was a location allotted, a task to perform; there was in fact, some part of the glory of this adventure.

"And my vision of the charts showed me that there was a line there for me. In my egotism I saw the line as central – mistakenly it appeared to stand out from all the rest. And the line began in some distant area and progressed through the project, it changed its nature as I myself changed; and my functions were then displayed, my requirements delineated, and my hopes expressed.

"And there were, too, those of the engineers who had been called upon to install the library's brilliant lights. These workers' lines were a wreathing, striding bundle. They had loops and smaller eddies. They set out from perhaps the interrogation rooms, met, whirled, performed every single function – over an extended period of time – and as the task became completed they moved apart – to more distant regions – and thus only a small fraction remained in their cyclic endeavour: restoring and repairing, maintaining bright lights.

"But my vision throughout had been restricted in the extreme. What I perhaps saw was only the smallest part of the truth – you have to remember my own limitations – and I am certain of course that my own perceptions and prejudices have dulled, coloured what is true.

"Nevertheless, a strong impression remains and the workers who have questioned me bear out the idea: at its very mention, they excitedly gesture, talk volumes in this way, and clearly the spirit of my dream spreads rapidly from them - and out to their fellows. So strong is the vision and the reason underlying it, that it seems impossible that only the past and present are to be enshrined in the charts in this way.

"And so it is true that futures are represented on the charts: that they are detailed plans, that the workers interpret them. But at this appraisal the eyes of my helpers have always dulled. 'No, no!' They have said, for it has somehow dissatisfied them.

"What I know *will* satisfy them is the reaction of the movement. For the great organization grows, it shifts and it changes: in the library intelligence is gathered and reports are made. These then are transmitted upward: they are directed straightaway towards the interpreting rooms.

"And so the charts – these are divided into sections, rolled up they are stacked round the walls of each room – the charts are then brought out, examined, at times they are amended; and they represent the whole patchwork of one single plane.

"At times tally clerks come and they verify which part of the plane is presently being examined – in each of the rooms – and between these individuals runners rapidly move, so approximately at least, a continuous check is maintained. And a line or a group of lines may shift from one chart to another, and the runners then move quickly, their vital information with them, and they cause new sections to be examined – in perhaps remote rooms – and every part of the movement is represented in this way and every function too, and at any time then the workers, their tasks, pasts, presents and futures . . ."

And suddenly I saw all of this – the level upon level – it was a moment of clarity: an intuitive step of which any interpreter would be proud.

". . . They are all here described." So that Ruth's vision then included the shifts and the changes: "It includes," she said, "the adjustments that have to be made."

But the sparkling moment passed fleetingly on. It moved, was sought for secretly, and I quickly forgot this newest power. Ruth continued:

"With the reports," Ruth's body moved easily – every gesture struck home – "which come from the library, the interpreters commence the modifications to the charts. These are shifts in policy. They represent responses to the progress within the movement and developments outside.

"Even so, it is clear that this great responsibility is not to be carried out lightly. The progress of the adjustments, the people involved, all are exactly detailed in the charts from the start; and so throughout there is only a certain diffuse responsibility. The onus for change is upon the movement itself. And there are no leaders within our ranks, and no prior knowledge either. The originators themselves are legends – perhaps now imitated – and what is now left to us is the growing organic structure within. And no one now would interfere with the power of the idea, for this now transcends understanding - and the comprehension even of its makers.

"And we are to be grateful too, to the early discoverers of processes capable of generating even *themselves*. Grateful, too, for developments in graphics enabling the diagrams to be displayed in such a permanent form as these charts. Though the details of the central scheme itself can, naturally, only be partially understood, what *is* certain is that nearly every discipline within the university has at some time been involved in the development of the central ideas. These grow and develop within – as models of the origin of life; of the engendering of consciousness or the flow of human and even animal need. And we are confident that everything encountered by the growing project has its analogue within, for all the efforts of the workers are aimed at informing this centre - and adapting the response displayed by interpreters working with the charts. And the university itself is grateful for the light this movement has been able to throw on many aspects of its own research. Such central, simple and overwhelming ideas can only have had their origin, they say, in the most elementary of propositions – in the knowledge (as with organic life itself) that the whole is greater than the part or that all beings are directed towards the reproduction of their own kind.

"And such developments could not have been foreseen during the days in which the project spontaneously arose . . . But then my vision suddenly shifted: in the eyes of a dear interpreter I saw his special love for the project. The interpreter's eyes were surely those of a guardian of the truth so that when gestures from within the library indicated that changes had to be made – he was, perhaps, accommodating you within the adventure – I saw that he acted with an awareness of our destiny: there was thus always a harmony of interest. His acts were benign. (All the interpreters who work in teams have been informed of your arrival. If not already anticipated, your presence and your progress will have been recorded in the charts.) And when your assigned helper makes a report – in your case, possibly, interrogator Laura – then this process begins, and by means of the combined wisdom, not just your past becomes detailed but essentially too – invention, aspiration, the sense of all consequences. Your future and our aims, the whole rich and patterned life becomes apparent.

"But the charts are formed on different planes and I have heard occasionally of certain higher ones still. And other possibilities exist – and can therefore cause great happiness – so that when the interpreters work, four to a room amid heat, noise, the efforts and disturbance of the others, then it may actually be that a yet higher chart is being consulted and perhaps partially interpreted so that the glory of all other probabilities is made plain – and the movement is thus elevating and worthy of our hope.

"And to this fine aspiration you may yet be invited!"

So I did perhaps understand the meaning of Ruth's vision. Certainly, the evident response of the movement implied the truth of her interpretation. Dissatisfaction with lesser possibilities meant that they, the bright souls involved, must of necessity, respond in precisely this way.

Yet further questions still arose: I could see that group imperfections persisted – channels of command were obscure, perhaps even faulty – the painters who had fallen from the earliest of heights, still had asked *me* if I had come with any instructions . . .

But Ruth showed clearly that this great project worked – worked in spite of such failures – and that the reason for the fall of Christopher and David could only have been that they had not succeeded for themselves.

By the same token Ruth made no claims at all for herself. She described not a single detail of her past nor anything of her future. Her explanation of how she arrived at this level could contain none of the movement's apparent insight: her memory was faulty like each early member whom she had ever seen.

So, although it was possible for Ruth to name each region she had visited within the movement, there was now no significance to the wide-eyed and girlish impression that she would be able to give and clearly she meant I ought therefore to dispense straightaway with all such irrelevances.

Ruth got up. With great deliberation she picked up every one of her clothes.

CHAPTER NINE

We moved towards the door. The obstruction – it was Roger's form - shifted. His eye, pressed to the crack in the doorway, moved and he stepped out of our way. I gripped the door handle and let the light flood in.

A frenzy of gestures greeted us as we walked towards the desk where Roger, a clerk once more was now seated. A sudden question occurred to me on approaching his place in the light.

But Ruth caught this thought which might otherwise have escaped, fluttered, and sped throughout the library:

"You cannot expect signs of any one particular nature," she said, answering my question before it was even properly formed.

Immediately, Roger sensing some collusion began in a hesitant way to produce a formal speech:

"Interruptions – caused by you – in the work of the library have been noted and passed on.

"Our friend Ruth is no longer suitable as our . . ." he paused, baulking at the word *interpreter*, until finally settling upon the word *go-between*, and then stammering as the unhappy simile became suddenly apparent to him. ". . . And I will arrange for someone else . . ." He moved his hands then, but Ruth was not to be put off so readily.

Gesturing fiercely at first and then gradually with a more gentle sway of her body – this became at once reptilian and enticing – she told Roger of her need to see understanding between all her paramours and she brushed aside his objections with sensuous movements each of which bordered upon the caress. Ruth had obviously introduced whole new gradations into the language of gestures. Her worth to the movement was never more apparent.

Under such sweet rhythms Roger was able to wave aside the clerk who now stood in front of him, sending him to his seat once more. It was possible, his expression said, that there might be shades of meaning in the following interview which might deserve the touch that Ruth alone could bring. At this, of course, Ruth smiled benignly.

I started to feel that this small figure could not possibly command the respect of all within the movement. If it had not been for the obvious delight with which Ruth received the pressure of his fingers upon her, I would have shouted out right there amid the library silence that such contact was surely unnecessary and that the language of gestures did not require Roger's hand to mingle with hers – and in the area of intimacy, too.

But I did not, and in the following silence Roger explained that on each occasion when he had had to hammer on the door, he had found it necessary to request that the work of the library be halted, this for fear that errors might be made during the period of disturbance. Each such disturbance had had to be incorporated into the work of the library and so into the fabric of the movement itself. The degree of disruption was exactly calculable. Clearly he meant that I would be held responsible for it. Roger's formal speech continued:

"I was distressed to think our progress might be impeded by certain misconceptions you appear to have about my status within the movement." And Ruth, explaining all of this, was now bent low and was whispering into my ear. Roger, distracted, was thus able to run his hands over the soft and yielding body that I loved.

"Apparently," he began, "you are lamentably out of touch with our affairs. I know you even feel I am somehow ill-qualified to . . ."

"Oh no! I'm sure he doesn't think that!" Ruth spoke out loud. For my benefit she dropped all tactile communication. Spurning the gestures, for once she turned Roger's probing hand away.

"I do so want us to be friends!" She said. "Then I can be happy!

"Tell him about the guards then he'll understand. He'll see how important you are then!"

Roger warmed.

Yes, to describe the guards would certainly be useful. It would serve truth; would bring Ruth, Roger and myself closer together, and would serve equally as a gesture of accommodation towards the work of the library.

Roger prepared himself for the task. His hands fluttered; he tested several opinions, and only when a small measured agreement became apparent did he speak and then with collective authority and his own quite evident, naked and urgent need.

Roger began: "The guards are responsible for manning the barricades. Their influence extends beyond the cordon however, and so we often have to work with the help of many other people. This is a feature of the organization: individuals and groups with special duties in one area are not permanently restricted to that particular location. In this way, it is only to be expected that the guards do not merely hover on the perimeter of the movement, never to be admitted to the secure inner regions . . ." Roger's use of the word *secure* puzzled me.

" . . . And so the presence of the guards extends far into Dunelm House. It is in this way that the guards operate well within . . . and so we are involved in policy-making for the whole - on many, many levels."

He paused.

"And of this decision-making body, I am the head." The pride was evident – he explained his position further. So great was his need, he explained his position within the library.

"I am – it has to be admitted – in a junior position within this library. It is only to be expected, therefore, that I am not party to every aspect of the work here. It has been due to my efforts within the guards that I have been invited to deal with matters of security at this, the more elevated level. Nevertheless, even this small foothold where beautiful ideas operate represents a considerable step up. Such is my responsibility, and one of which I hope you are now fully aware."

Ruth nodded encouragement to this. "It is for this reason I am not able fully to explain the work that is done here. But rest assured there will be many others who will show a firmer grasp of the principles involved."

Ruth nodded again. She made it quite clear that the rapprochement was very important indeed as with a grin which I wanted to think of as sheepish, Roger made a lunge for Ruth and held her. He made it equally clear how much his explanation would now cost. Ruth smiled once more – it was a disturbing lack of resignation.

So the library was a repository. I understood that instructions came down from the interpreting rooms and as new intelligence blossomed from among the silences, the whispered words and gestures of the interrogators, a dialogue grew up. As new intelligence came from the organization outside – the organic, spreading reach of the movement – so policy shifted. It was, of course, interpreters who knew of the relevant facts.

I was shocked. That the structure should grow was inevitable. And I visualised a nebulous body of information gatherers: Christopher and David – those small sparks playing among the gravestones; Christopher and David who had compounded a doctor's attention, had distracted his patient, later drawing him on to unaccustomed regions. Regions where he might falter and fail – fail like a pendulum at the end of its swing. And I saw that such a body would swarm voluptuously, would ingest all that came before it just as simultaneously such minute and flashing lights would dart outward, would test and sample, would inform a growing centre. And so the guesswork and the worthy official opinion flooded in – flooded in as a rapid and tropical growth – and the streams met, circled about each other and then headed on: one for the centre and one always outward – outward to the town, the university - through the dank air of the vennels - and to other places disguised at times as light and airy.

And there were fresh and timorous faces in the interrogators' cubicles. There were projects which had been finished before their time, and there were schedules not yet begun. There were interrogators, guards; and bright faces, too, in the library of shining light.

It was here that the interpreters came to be briefed; here, too, their leaders met so that they might make their reports, be inspired by inner contact and receive renewed instructions. Surely, I thought, this must be the seat of the developing power of the idea?

But Roger continued: he was talking quite excitedly now, he described the interrogators – those working in the field – and he reminded me of how they ran the interrogations and he was definite – once more – about the need, if ever the grand design were to grow, for copious intelligence. He spoke of this as a natural precaution but he meant really to suggest to us both the air of the rarefied interpreting rooms, to draw a picture of the interpreters themselves and to enthuse over the elegant work that remained for them to do.

But Roger was dissatisfied with the result. He called it a naïve appraisal. He showed great unhappiness at his own inadequacy and it was only when Ruth, sensing despair, encouraged him with obscene and feminine wiles that he regained his enthusiasm to talk about anything at all. He raised what was, at that moment, the most important thing to him: he spoke of Ruth's and my stay in the darkened cupboard.

"I am disturbed," he began, "by the glaring inaccuracies in what Ruth had to say. I was compelled to interrupt you – the cause of the movement's truth was too dear to let the moment pass – I therefore clutched at the only way possible in which to stop the stream of hurtful untruths.

"My hammering . . ," he indicated the glistening and shimmering assembly, "was very disturbing – the disruption in the work alone is incalculable. We will be affected by its consequences until . . . until . . . ."

Ruth stepped in: "But you wanted to say?"

"Ah, yes!" He said, turning to me. "You have missed the significance of the phenomenon of parallelism. The charts – the parallel charts – took up barely a minute of Ruth's time. She omitted the multitude of other possible analyses; she ignored the higher charts and the profoundest of systems to which they refer, and thus she omitted to mention that in these charts and on rare occasions even you and I could be expected to figure; that such correspondences bring the individual into touch with perhaps the finest of causal areas and that to protect such regions desperate measures are often required. Witness my urgent hammering; the way I put at risk all the work of the library and, indeed, the willing sacrifice of my own secure and precious peace of mind."

Thus Roger collapsed back into silence and into his

consolation: once more his hands felt the softness of the body that I loved for I was to be held accountable for all that had gone before, and Ruth, whispering at last into my ear that I was indeed cut off from the movement's affairs, translated at last Roger's indignation, his anger at my presumption of his inadequacy, and continued in this way until she was forced to cry out – in response to his intimate penetration – for she actually shouted, she shouted out loud:

"Oh, no! I'm sure he doesn't think that!"

For Ruth spurned the language of gestures; she turned Roger's hands aside and, crying that she too sought happiness, she enticed Roger's interest by feigning a degree of concern.

What Roger said next was disturbed by a low and distant tolling. The bell sounds rumbled through the air finally to disturb every effort at normal speech: and now something more had to be remiss, for the sound plucked at me and with ecclesiastical assistance I became drawn, it lead me on:

"Come!" It said.

And once again more clearly:

"Come!"

And so Roger's face became alarmed, and his voice became drowned out and he continued – to do his duty, to make fine gestures; to talk reprovingly to me. And in all of this he was aided by Ruth. Ruth who was his private interpreter, Ruth, the brilliant star of the library of shining light, Ruth, now dancing – lightly – with a breeze from the doorway, dancing indeed to the bell's distant charms: Ruth, swaying in time, Ruth beginning with regular and haunting movements to fill my mind and those of all librarians. To fill our minds still.

And her grace was hard to bear and the uncompromising lights bore down on our faces while the same light, casting harsh shadows, made Ruth's face more fluid, it became more distinct and her limbs shone out brightly, her smile more sweetly, for it was a glistening dance, filled with iridescence, filled lightly with pain and our unworthy desire.

The bell tones became seductive and they merged with my love. It was an excellence blinding my sight and now I follow grotesquely. I dance with circles far beyond the library – and corridors marred with green and brown – and I go far from the ululation of the luminous host and those who gesture continually, are occupied into the far distance with the cares of an island universe – one among many.

And I am far away, I cry out. I discard to the circling winds my thoughts, my timorousness, friendship's cadences and those former fears: I am surrounded! By dull and ephemeral hues, by days misspent and my own incomprehension.

I see green.

So that it is the river that swirls by and everything is butted by the current: the wooden slats, the tailboard; and is fixed by the twisting lantern gaze and I at last emerge to dry my hair, to cast out detritus and the hope in others' eyes. I am to be free while a crowd cries out; as I evolve – rapidly – and with honeyed approval, Ruth continues to dance. To my steps she adds her rhythms and they are soon adopted; swept up by the crowd. It is the host of the gilded ones, the light-filled librarians.

They begin to incant:

"Oh come!"

They shout and they move within the cathedral's thrall, "Come!" So that some part beckons me on and it is a pageant of discord: shapes and shadows and Ruth in brilliant hues.

The bell: "We give Thee thanks!" And it tolls again.

"We give Thee thanks – Almighty God – for Thy great glory!"

And I will be accused of sins of omission, commission, and the sins of the thought.

And so once again: "We give Thee thanks!"

I see green which is now the colour of the rowing eight – it dominates the earth-brown – and in the absence of Christopher, the gravedigger, it is David who approaches though others would have liked to. They would have whispered low and perhaps with menace; they would have moved close and frozen something that is dear. One by one they would have torn at me, but only David was qualified, only David knew what to say, only David had a tale to tell.

And so he leans upon me – the one with the fearful experience to relate; the one buoyed up by the horror; the one who can foresee the increase that the bearing of a story to my, yes, my ears might have.

"I was walking just as you are now . . ." He began. "It was dark and I had difficulty in seeing my way." I turned to look at him for at that moment there was still a certain rancour in my bearing. I was pondering his strange audacity.

"Forgive me!" He said, noticing my irritation – a certain aloofness which has often clothed me.

"It may not be an exact parallel – I was engaged upon a journey, nothing more. Perhaps the resemblance ends there for I did not know my goal nor even the place where my journey might end."

He gestured now in the familiar and disturbing language of gestures; he drew a fine distinction, a precious difference between one's destination and the actual end of one's journey.

And yet alone, David was to find the approach difficult. Without the wind and the rain – those inhabitants of graveyards – he would be strangely alone, over-extended. In fact, perhaps their loss was affecting him unaccountably for I know neither my own destination nor where my journey might end. But the tale bore him up. When he faltered, the sway of his arms, the tilt of his hands carried him onwards. It was almost as if the story grew from the rhythms of his body – a fictional act and the more significant for being the product of his own quite delicate form.

"It was night," he said, "when I began my walk and at first I had a companion. He was rather unwelcome. Very soon after the beginning of our journey he disappeared. The most significant act that he was capable of therefore was accomplished at the very start. His success is to be admired, is it not?

"For me the walk consisted in paces dulled by wet grass: the grass that grows muddily by the side of a road. Paces and a constantly lightening sky. But I was not to remain alone for long. I was visited by fearful ideas throughout the night, some of them taking on forms unaccountably strange: strange in an air stirred and shaken by my own presence. Somehow the events of that night required that I should, in fact, *be there* – for in this way the traveller induces a reaction so that making such a journey becomes a passive activity. Indeed, you would do well to bear this in mind. Perhaps it was because I was unaware of this fact that I saw my pool of evil. (Such a pool was a shimmering and faintly luminous disc that floated perhaps a foot above the ground. It thus blocked my path and reduced me to a helpless inactivity.)

"I have told this story to many people. Some, and there are those who carry some authority – as I did once – have given it a moment of their time but they have always ended up by asking me to describe certain details either of the walk which I took or of the apparition which filled me with such horror.

"I believe that the details of my journey are not important at all. My reason for setting out and even the appearance of this vision are all but irrelevant too. Equally true is the fact that a traveller's intended destination and the view others might have of his undertaking might differ widely. And so it is that I have refused to answer these questions and the others to whom I might speak have, in their frustration, brought about my downfall from the position of eminence to which I have alluded. Consequently the outcome of the journey has been very different from anything that has yet been proposed to me. While at the same time calling me truculent and obsessively secretive, they have used this as an excuse to work all kinds of vengeance upon me.

"Only I can see that a strange redundancy among the night's events is the only real interpretation of my journey and for this reason the way it reacted upon me is crucial. My passivity, the way that this insight was to bring about the annoyance of others and consequently my changed position; these were the true goals of my walk. Some of this might have been known at the outset, but the important thing is that the walk reflected upon those characteristics which have been outlined to you. It has been a harrowing but truly wonderful experience to perceive such a mechanism of destiny. I am truly glad that perhaps I did once set out upon my journey, though now, of course, I am not at all sure that I ever did."

At this final word shouting broke out. As each familiar face in the crowd clamoured for his explanation to be heard, David's face took on a menaced look – for he was standing next to me and the violent shouting had spread. It was like a disease regarded by some as unpleasant, perhaps even dangerous. And the gesturing became wild; it became awesome – itself an adventure.

But in the end David succumbed to his problems for now that his tale was over he had increasing difficulty in holding onto my side. He was buffeted unhappily until, losing his foothold and becoming dislodged, he left me in the middle of a group of figures each of whom maintained his position near to the centre only by means of an extreme effort.

Rapidly, David became obscured by this crowd until only a wildly gesticulating arm remained to be absorbed – and that appeared to come from a spot which was so near the ground, that its owner could not be in anything but a kneeling position. Twice more David was to break free from his tormentors, but without his story to back him up he found his confidence failing him – and this before he had crossed more than a few feet of the gap between the boldest of the crowd and myself.

In the meantime, the others were making themselves heard. Throughout, the phrase *mechanism of destiny* seemed important in what they had to say, for although no two explanations seemed to agree, nevertheless the theme of personal destiny apparently occupied the speakers almost completely; indeed I was alarmed at the vehemence with which the gesticulating figures pressed this very point.

Among their number stood Reverend Ashley apparently leading this most angry of crowds. Suddenly, a sound rose which had once been architectural, but now that he was in the open was free and full of terrible wrath. It was only with great difficulty that he restrained the figures – their accusations becoming extravagant – so that all the time the priest intoned his elegant creed, their cry was of:

"Turncoat!"

And again, "Deceiver!"

And finally, "Murderer!"

But it was the priest who turned aside these denunciations. The tolling of the cathedral bell was not able to distract him; nor the strange and magnetic force which drew him onwards. I began to recognize the strength of such a man who could, at a time like this, calmly discuss yet one more explanation for the story of the journey – and indeed, show conclusively how this explanation was suited to our present destination. (We stepped beyond the oak doors: we were outside Dunelm House. We were joined by the crowd of librarians – missing their revealing luminescence – we were part of their misshapen pageant: the vennel faces and certain strange, rotund and glistening forms.)

"The fact that we are discussing the matter at length shows that this itself must be part of the journey's goal. Indeed, the fact that we are distracted by this – David's act – clearly indicates its significance and his complicity. Yet he too is unable to approach except when armed with just this story: the account of a walk, undertaken we are told, on a night when rain made the grass wet, wet and muddy under foot."

But I who had become the centre of this discussion, I who felt threatened by this cold interpretation, I, their deceiver, cried out that here the matter had become exaggerated – that the truth now was impossible to fathom. I cried out among the deafening boom of the cathedral's bell, that here was no justice, no justice at all!

But the unjust crowd moved on, it murmured all around me. The sound of voices struck deepest terror inside me, for from far behind I caught sight of hideous forms, saw those open-faced librarians; and I saw their companions – they were the ill-shapen ones that the shadows tended to become. I felt at once they would clutch for me fearlessly, that their collective sighings, their breathing – which is the hopeless esperance from every mountain top – these feigned sounds would fill me with heavy menace, disillusionment. And there are pinched and whitened faces; they have stared at me fiercely, and they are even now seen at this town's street corners.

But the cathedral stands before us to save us from too much disquiet – and its shadow will fall happily across all of us. It will cut out the harsh light and we will pass gently from vennel crossing places; certain quiet respites from today's bright sun.

My steps reverberate and suddenly everything is cold. It is the wind. Having found something to say, it does so brutally, it is cold tearlessly. A cry shrieks from the throats of the throng and the priest incants once more so as to separate the travellers' sounds and my own discordant paces.

The harsh light is now totally gone. The sun is blocked off. The organ draws us on with tones which shake the earth at our feet and I look up to see the sculptured and leprous faces of the saints, the effigies in cornices of the wall, saints and the more hideous gargoyles: the shapes of the fellow travellers. The arch of the doorway lies ahead, dulled roseate forms in the windows; worn stonework, weather-rounded corners and the stone flags of the path through the graveyard which ring to our paces dissonantly.

The bell tolls again – a powerful intimacy like the gentle and delicate bump of a liner as it touches first the quay, then stands off by a matter of inches; a great weight poised there. (There are bell sounds too, from above, and a tower which cuts off the sun.)

My accusers, those that survived the river and a host of once friendly faces are near to the entrance. They are no longer to be restrained, they pause only momentarily. They follow me into the depths of the cathedral. The procession flinches: I in despair; while from behind a light holds all of us enthralled – my own figure and certain travellers. But straightaway the priest has made for the open crypt. I see the glint of brightly lit torches; livid flames. And in the corners of the reredos, the candlesticks, flames flicker. The figures surround the tomb's open mouth, the heap of its fresh earth, the discarded flagstones and an excavated stairway.

The light stabs towards darkness. This hides shortly behind each column, hides there that is, until discovered; darts then suddenly to another pillar and thus the threat lies beyond the sight and menaces always at the edge of one's vision.

Steps worn by pilgrims lead to oak doors which are cast wide. In place of those inner regions where beauty might have been found I am swept on to darkness. I am rejected. Clearly unwelcome. But I am to be made joyful at the happy suggestion whispered to me by one of my companions, that perhaps here the adventure has gained a foothold; perhaps, in fact, the cathedral is not beyond the pale. Possibly, too, these green-clad vergers, like early converts to the work itself, perhaps these too, are occasionally to be found among honest toilers from within.

And if this is so, then the lesson which David learned could equally be relied upon and thus the journey to the centre might prove to have a very different outcome from the one anticipated. For the circle which is so large that its circumference is at infinity must have a ubiquitous centre and all journeys in search of this goal must finish where they set out; that all locations must inevitably be identical, and that all places are, and always have been, identical with the very centre itself.

But there was something more besides – and the smooth, flat surface was icy, white. Grey, the sky reached down to this flat plane: featureless. It formed the circle. And beneath it, unawares, there was power, imagination. Just as a sea mammal might, with inimitable strength, nose its way up, might force its way through the ice-sheet. Or else with a fine, shrew-like snout it might find some chink, some fissure – an inconsistency which by meticulous and painful probing it might cause to widen; widen that is until the whole form, the whole steaming life-mass might lie gloriously on the snow-clad plain. There it would glisten wet in the sun and at last fill my thoughts with its fine, living, wild and free, perhaps terrifying sweet form. I turned to diligence, application:

To those workers, those charts – pored over by groups of four – and the chaos and the language of gestures. I remembered that the charts formed layers – superimposed upon each other – I remembered a line might disappear from one to reappear at another and I remembered the chilling question Roger had put before leaving the library:

"What sort of reality," he had suddenly asked, "might conceivably be represented by the thirtieth or even the third such parallel chart?"

My blood ran icily. For the sea's rare beast had not yet risen to flop magnificently out onto the clean surface, had not yet broken the fragile ice-world upon which I lay.

Just then singing began. It filled every part of me. Candles flickered and cast the priest's shadow onto the stonework inside the nave. They distorted the living being. They cast it onto the cold alcoves; the wooden pews and the fragmentary fine decorations; the smaller features.

Beyond the nave, between the columns and the walls, echo the steps of the dark wanderers – though the light which struggles through the spaces between these columns cannot catch even the slightest part of these figures, so that night stretches outward and there are eyes concealed in the infinite region beyond the nave.

I sat in an allotted place and I watched the vergers rush as they carried now a candelabrum, now a paten: all of which glittered in the little light, till somehow the company melted away. There was some concourse between the staring forms, in recesses, but it was hardly to be heard at the centre – in the halo of light from the few candles, at the open crypt amid the dust of the crypt amid, too, the hint and the silence of death.

And I knelt in this light, and I sought among the shadows for quietly moving forms; for a familiar, friendly, less fevered face till I felt, quite suddenly, that I should not, in my own best interest, stray from this spot. There were others unseen but sometimes moving; quietly pacing among the shadows. Darting now from behind grey columns – and passing nearby so that I heard the soughing of their garments, the hollow sounds of their breathing and the heartbeat of their intent.

And there was a moment like this for the lonely one: a silent and emptied, a twisting figure in the river. The figure who was unable to complete any action and certainly found it difficult to look fixedly at anyone so that his eyes ranged instead over a fine assembly. A figure whose eyes searched among the crowd for strange shapes: the forms among the trees that resembled the trees and which stalked this lonely figure; had especially followed him for longer than he knew and had clutched for him – as he drifted with the river – and had at last caught rapturously his dying, sweet, his violent essence.

Stephen and I shared this outcome of fate for there are those who have plucked at me and now that huddled shapes are seen to pursue me – I who am blinded by whatever I wish – I become a shadow, an incompetent, a half-life, a half-man. Stephen's gaze had twisted then among the crowd; had sent dead stabs outward and these – like a searchlight had found what indeed was strange and not to be counted among ordinary men. All unwittingly his eyes had lit upon the rare ones: those who are shapeless – who pursue and are pursued – the creatures of the reckoning, reckoning strangers, the travellers, the unbridled, the reckoning few.

And where was the consolation? Where were the gentle eyes that had tempted and which mine had caressed? Where was the rounded, sweet, soft and loving form which had driven me on and brought me naked into the region; had driven the vision of the wall from my eyes: had set at nought a stony contemplation when Theo was at my side? Clearly, icily, all fond hope faded for consolation could not exist while the irretrievable fault remained – ignorance of one's failings – and it could only be that such answers as were possible might eventually be obtained by extreme and painstaking self-enquiry so, by this means alone might I rise above consolation and partial forms; above fear, above sad arabesques. I would then float freely in the upper air. Erect, self-reliant, I would take on the colours of the sun itself.

But Theo and Peter are not here, nor must I seek them further. I have been in error in so many ways and my passage down corridors within has been marred by intentions of which no one could approve – as I made my way along corridors of increasing aberrance, the interrogators warned me of the danger of seeking friends at all. This advice, however, as always, had gone unheeded.

And advice came too from Ruth, the dearest of my tormentors. From this brilliant and elusive star had come the same warning and so threatening a shining, erect, self-reliant and free form were the hidden faults which in their subtlety and concealment must indeed lie forever unknown. I, who left unheeded the warnings of my brightest hope must therefore expect to remain forever excluded.

But at times a hopeless striving can be put to good use. There are times when the sought-for solution is in fact close at hand. David who had been vilified had yet achieved something – his tale – and must now possess such insight that these former injustices can matter hardly at all.

Yes, the river was far away and Stephen's twisting gaze: it too was distant. And the imperfections and the sad impurities need seek no further justification. For all these things – the individual acts of cowardice, the lonely moments of failure, the pride – all were now one; quietly they had become justified as I held onto the single shining example of David and his moment of ecstasy. I saw now the crushed form left hollowly by the crowd – and from his mouth he repeated with his incessant lips and with his final gasp, his own special, dark, lean and tragic tale.

I turned to penetrate the cathedral's recesses. In these darknesses – behind the tapestries, the hangings concealing quite as much as they were able to display; behind them in the darkness I caught sight of certain movement. For decidedly, I was surrounded by more than just the stone which rang for me, the choir's concordance and the rustle of the celebrant's vestments. And yet it was entirely possible to dismiss the whole proceedings, the entire fabric, as tenuous, hardly substantial – and rising from my pew to walk out and into the slight breeze . . . but there is a peril behind such infinite subtlety of the fault; there is one more danger – that I could dismiss too much.

And Ruth did exist. These eyes had seen her undulation; I had heard the adherents' ululation and had proved ready, even, for work in the library. And so before this cathedral service was even ready I must have failed in something very real, for why else was it demanded that I undergo this searching, questioning, this examining – and it was especially necessary: it was an act of compulsion and it spread outward from certain staring eyes to be seen now among the columnar shadows.

This then represented the crux: the gravest error of all. My forehead beaded; my head rolled this way and that as phantasms rose and torments began. Was it, after all, Stephen's death? Had this warrior not recognized some figment of this terrible last exigency? And there had been a frightening change too when the dark overtook the splendour of the librarians so, as I looked about me, I could see that many once familiar faces were transformed in the dimness and half-light and in many such cases, grotesques were the inevitable outcome.

I felt more involved in this furthest flung reach of the adventure than ever I had before. Suddenly, a familiar face – one that peered perhaps from the trees beside the river – the river had been heavy with mist – moved forward and hurried, burdened, towards the altar. In spite of the weight to be carried, this figure held himself erect: he was light-limbed, a youth with the blessing of the white sun on his face and the straining light from the rose window above picked at his features – those of a man from Hatfield College, and I knew as he importantly fixed me with his glance he was indeed my messenger, an object of my search – my own private hope.

And so I was to meet, at last, this sweetness – my route had not therefore been a meandering one – and I thought of Ruth's explanation of her labyrinthine path; of the meeting in the library and of her dismissal – rightly – of the minutiae of her journey and of the circle which is infinite and of the colouring, the character, the endless refinement of the traveller's soul.

The images which rose before me were necessary now – they were coloured bright hues; they were perhaps green. They were forceful and they overshadowed something cold, a thing frightfully to be remembered; an object to the search.

I felt I understood him. Without the merest sound he indicated the presence of every one of my pursuers and equally showed that though I would not now meet them, Theo and Peter, in an alcove or a dim recess were, as always, silently looking on. I understood suddenly a search might thus end in the acquisition of its goal, while at the same time the very demands which originally prompted the search might yet remain completely unfulfilled.

I looked at the messenger's back. So much had been conveyed by the economy of his gestures – the walk out of the darkness behind me, the burden, the set of his shoulders, that it flashed before me: here was a true communication, that Ruth could be proud a little and pleased once more.

"You cannot hope to understand!" And the flashing of a single hand indicated a future journey – a horrible odyssey – and it induced a dark vision: myself spinning onwards, so that I began to look at this future with the vertigo of a dying man contemplating eternity.

"For none of us do!

"Not the elms . . ." and the mention of the strange word, the odd resounding name of tall trees; the sound, here in the cathedral was welcome, unexpected, but truly in order. And the priest made his way, and the choir swept steadily nearer and a wind arose, slamming doors and windows, and clouds dulled the bright and occasional, the final day.

And it was on this day I had met the messenger. On this day, Theo and Peter in the shadows; Ruth too. And I stepped toward the altar; to the candle light, the flickering light, and the rust-red, earth-lit, sanctified and open tomb and the singing then rose and my breath came hard and I knelt at the altar-rail: a bright communion.

A communion of souls: desires, the end and an acquisition. And radiance gathered round me. The colours, glistening, become supporting. To the smile of the messenger I am to rise, become insubstantial. Beneath, where the blackness and cold figures impress, circles swirl and night moves in eddies.

Will the burden allow it and can anyone disagree? The burden lies heavily. The grotesques can be fully seen so cathedral and adventure express some slight human will.

I must float up. Levels slip by, some giddying ascent and dream – the hues of other characters form slightly all around; their radiance can cause more brilliance and the tomb is now filling, arcs come from below. And below.

The friends can come too. At some heights and other areas sensation gives way. Their closeness – warmth, friendship, light and their love – they vibrate, rainbow sight. They are near: ascent beyond mine. They are here quite risen and some part penetrates, persists. Some strange and glaring birth has been invoked.

So the adventure is a fine expression. And within the distant, intriguing corridors and the hollow spaces and busy halls, among the whispering and the comfort of human warmth, with slight or gentle tempering comes forth hope: my thoughts' rare abandonment. Adventure and friends shine: replicas of one's slight hope. In some glowing spark, ember, is this arc's beginning. They spread, upward, coloured, outward: they suggest awesome regions and then discoveries. I must look down to the crypt.

The messenger approaches, everyone gathers breath. The representation of some ignoble death can now cause the great sighings and the soughing; and beyond the grey, noble pillars strange dances may be begun. Faces there are here. And I have seen these images, have held their cold gaze quietly. In the river and by the low-water sounds there have been figures that danced silently – with the wind and the driven rain, the circle dance too. The figures plucked, called forth obscenely, they now cry out sickeningly, they reach out for life. And now the dance gathers speed. As the pageant circles, the wind whistles in the nave's depths. The abandoned, the revelling, the hurtful dark travellers stamp disconsolately in time. Their paces echo and ring. From the vaulting, the candle chandeliers, the sound of dull cries drop, fall to every side altar; the night's small procession now girdles the church.

Thus they fill the cathedral – where but in the small halo of candles might I thus be? It can be viewed from above.

Priest, messenger, burden and crypt. I must look at the faces. Certain, at one time, among the dark revellers – Laura; a few other friends; perhaps the suggestion of Stephen. These suck for my life. The slightest of glimpses is to occur. The misshapen ones form into parts, at times recognisable. There, surely, Christopher's gesture of disdain? And as the dancers supplicate and then feint, a whole pattern can be seen that glances, shadows, evasions cannot conceal; and at some point therefore, wisdom, true aid, comfort and friendship will be at hand.

And the ceremony proceeds: the precise, delicate communication founded in beauty – the gestures of all the figures and those, once light-filled, that are disconsolate and dance in the outer deep reaches.

In time with the priest's gestures, the grotesque host trembles – at times this is a resonance: it seems to flicker sympathetically. Variously, it seems repulsed. The priest makes bold gestures – all fall back at a pace.

But, too, in eagerness they move rapidly to the light. At these times, the candles' light flickers. The wind which is circling is raised in gusts. This threatens the single delicate haven.

The ceremony is strange. The actions, the rite, become distorted in the extreme. At times a rare familiarity is predominant, at others when threats or the glory of ascendance become recognized these forms become renewed and no slight resemblance to living, dead, or any human precept is maintained.

This glory is then a brilliant and lucid expression. The desires, the majesty of its characters suggest gradations. The ceremony is strange. Strange, too, unexpected, totally unjustified – my involvement, even, and my central crucial role. The gestures are totally unknown. What passes between the hordes and the figures in the light ebbs and flows and its depth and darkness spin me off in fright.

The cold image is involved – the burden, the crypt, the dark forces beyond. I feel I must depart. As the sounds rise – the choir, whose secular chants join wind, rain, the howling of travellers, I ascend and am removed from the incomprehensible faults and I drift up to bright friends and strange, warm life above.

Bells chime again, a cathedral statue reflects the light.

PART THREE

CHAPTER TEN

And there was a final silence. From above, from the walls of the cathedral, moistness glistened. Mosses dampened the coldness, the wind-blown coldness; the rain and the wind-blown, the lonely prominences. A cornice face, remote and weathered, stares in place of all sanctity and the lichen masses delicately over the encrusted features, barren features.

Within, in the intervals between the fluting – the stone traceries – flickers the light from the candles, desolately. For inside, where the wind only threatens there is no warmth: outside the figure stands in vigil, while inside there has always been the draught of the centuries. What the stone eyes have never seen are the shadows in the intervals, the transient ones, and the purple depths beyond the nave. And the eyes have been sightless throughout these years. The single and lonely visits have toyed with not a moment of rigid vision; the birds have nested, they have cried out unheedingly. And now the wind rises, it whips and fills the spaces while inside tall candles flicker. The light, stained, darkened by the windows, picks out the dust that has risen from the centuries, that has filled the cathedral air.

From where the birds mark at the windows, flutter, plucking at the light – it is yellowed, it is purpled – there are staffs which reach down to scratch at the altar. To scratch and lightly to discover gold.

From the doorway – the small stand and the velvet tables – from the clear day outside, light slopes to the stone flags: angled, parallel and forward, lightly to discover gold.

The eyes of an occasional visitor who might stand – awesomely – beside the stone staircase would look into the distance, gathering darkness about him – towards the open grave and the brilliance of the candelabra, and finally to discover gold.

The occasional visitor, resembling stone, would mount remote steps, would have passed by the crumbling brown, the upturned uneven soil – it is the tomb's exposure – a singular fantasy. The features – lined, illuminated – would pass by the candles and be gently altered, changed as the eyes moved in the searching, shifting; lightly to discover gold.

The stairs lead up twisting in the tower, and sounds fill out the creep of the masonry – to the river, towards the river, the whole cathedral shifts imperceptibly and is less secure, for it is thus that stone is liquid, fragile and impermanent.

And at once the birds feel the inconstancy. Suddenly they fly with downstroke wingstrokes thrust about them – and hard. The wind gusts too and the bird-whirring flies into the air, so that the towers are engulfed and the day is perfectly confused.

Something then is able to rise, to fill untroubled the space above the cathedral, to rise into the winds which pierce windows and prod at the occasional visitor, climbing to the towers. Climbing, while all about him is maze-like, is stone-channelled and branched so that not even the number of ascents is known and every tower is a nest of stairwells.

In the dark space below, the rose window – blinded by trees – beads glistening raindrops and the harsh winds scratch at a northern stonework, attack that which is vulnerable and leave – just the mortar.

The wind screams.

The darkness, hiding forms, stretches out beyond stone pillars. Fragile fingers darkly reach towards the altar, they reach and are repulsed, unable lightly to approach and all unseen, overwhelm its gold. And so, beyond the stone, untroubled face, the cathedral teems with an intricate darkness.

But there is something midway between the candle's half-light and the soughing of garments beyond the nave. Between the pillars, the saints of the side altars await whatever may befall. Their pause has lasted. They have stood there glinting now and then for eight centuries. They are the dust and the tallow, the praying and the striking of poses.

The sunlight fades in the space of the minutes or hours and reddens the white and black and the tiers of the keys which are white and black and the organ which is brown, sunlit. Does the occasional visitor penetrate here to where there is the slightest of movements? To the loft where a wind has rustled the papers into slight disarray, the wind and the circling air above; from the small window in the vaulted space - by occasional birds' nests set in the rafters, those stone fronds overhead?

No, the occasional visitor would not come here, would never see the sheet music piled high with the hymnals and which slightly rustles in this the slightest of breezes; and the stairs too: charged with the surprising sounds, the sound which ancient wood secretes – an alarming dissonance.

And the shadows creep forward. Though repulsed as shade yet night must win, must stretch as the shadows lengthen so that the territory of the half-seen and fully frightful, will such as death pick at its gold. Now is the time for all true and occasional forms – the equivocal visitor – to leave in haste, to quit and seek that which is home. For here it is frightful, for here all that has passed and seems to have passed – the eight hundred years and the candles' present flickering – all these things appear to fade. As each shadow lengthens, moments vanish and the vistas slip away.

What is left is not the night but the fear of the night. As fingers stretch out, they grasp – and fearsomely – and finally to discover: everything to be cold.

Books by the same author:

'Vertical Line'
'Hor'

Printed in Great Britain
by Amazon